Kris eased her hand into her pocket for her cell phone.

Pressing the 1 would speed dial 9-1-1.

But did 9-1-1 work out here? Was there even any reception? The weight of fear and helplessness gripped her stomach. Despite the cold, sweat dripped down her back.

If he took a single step toward her, she would spin around and run for her life—and risk the chance that she could get the back door open in time.

The intruder pushed back one side of his full-length coat and unclipped his own cell phone from his belt, keeping the gun trained on her. Without taking his eyes from her face, he hit a single speed dial button, then held the phone to his ear.

"This is Trace, Sheriff. I need you out here right away. I just caught another one of those vandals, and you won't want to let this one get away."

Books by Roxanne Rustand

Love Inspired Suspense

*Hard Evidence
*Vendetta
*Wildfire
Deadly Competition
**Final Exposure
**Fatal Burn

*Snow Canyon Ranch
**Big Sky Secrets

ROXANNE RUSTAND

lives in the country with her husband and a menagerie of pets, many of whom find their way into her books. If not at her part-time day job as a registered dietitian, writing at home in her jammies, or spending time with family, you'll probably find her out in the barn with the horses or with her nose in a book.

This is her twenty-second novel, and is the second book in the Big Sky Secrets series. Her first manuscript won a Romance Writers of America Golden Heart Award, and her second manuscript was a Golden Heart Award finalist. Since then, she has been an *RT Book Reviews* Career Achievement Award nominee in 2005, and won the magazine's award for Best Superromance of 2006.

She loves to hear from readers! Her snail address is: P.O. Box 2550, Cedar Rapids, Iowa 52406-2550. You can also find her at: www.roxannerustand.com, www.shoutlife.com/roxannerustand, or at her blog, where readers and writers talk about their pets: http://roxannerustand.blogspot.com/.

FATAL BURN
ROXANNE RUSTAND

Steeple
Hill®

Published by Steeple Hill Books™

STEEPLE HILL BOOKS

Steeple
Hill®

Recycling programs
for this product may
not exist in your area.

ISBN-13: 978-0-373-44380-2

FATAL BURN

www.SteepleHill.com

Printed in U.S.A.

For I know the plans I have for you,
declares the Lord,
plans to prosper you and not to harm you,
plans to give you hope and a future.
—Jeremiah 29:11

With heartfelt thanks to Cindy Gerard and
Kylie Brant. This series wouldn't exist
if not for our annual plotting retreat, and I treasure
our friendship more than words can say!

ONE

Kris Donaldson gripped the unfamiliar set of keys and stared down the winding lane leading to Wind Hill Ranch. It held at least a foot of snow, though far less than the heavy snowpack out in the open areas.

Dusk had crawled over the rugged Montana landscape during the long drive from Battle Creek, but she'd been caught up in her disturbing memories and hadn't noticed the fading light.

And now, with more snow falling and narrow, twisting mountain roads behind her, it was too late to turn back.

She shuddered as she stared over the massive fallen tree blocking access to the property, its roots rising like a tangle of snakes toward the sky.

The surrounding pine forest pressed in from all sides, looming fiercely overhead. From somewhere in the gloom came the eerie hoot of an owl, then the terrified cry of some small, unlucky creature.

Supposedly there was a house a half mile ahead, but

no welcoming security lights glimmered through the pine branches. And though the lawyer had promised to make sure the electricity had been restored, she now had her doubts.

"I should have stayed in Battle Creek tonight," she muttered under her breath as she tramped through the snow to circle the twisted roots of the tree.

Here, the underbrush was less dense than at the other end. Maybe…

Climbing back in her SUV, she slowly drove over the brush, scraping between two saplings, then angled past a jagged boulder. Despite the SUV's four-wheel drive, the tires spun on the sharp incline. But then they grabbed and the vehicle shot up onto the lane, fishtailing wildly for several heart-pounding seconds.

Once she had the vehicle under control, she put it in Park and rested her forehead on the steering wheel until her pulse stopped racing. Then she flipped on her headlights, slipped the gearshift into Drive again and slowly eased down on the accelerator and crept forward, the headlights swinging past an impenetrable wall of pines on either side of the road as she navigated the serpentine curves.

The forest abruptly opened up into a small meadow, and she drew in a sharp breath.

Ahead, through the veil of falling snow, lay an old, two-story log cabin with a covered porch stretching across the front. There appeared to be several buildings in back—barns of some kind, maybe. Split-rail fencing behind the house trailed off into the deepening twilight.

Not a ranch, really—just forty acres—but it was pretty as a Christmas card.

The portable dog kennel in the back of the SUV rattled, and her elderly golden retriever whined, scrabbling at the mesh door.

"Hold on, Bailey," she called out loudly enough for him to hear.

The dog barked a single acknowledgment that made her smile, thankful for his presence.

She'd camped alone in remote areas of the Rockies and Appalachians, and she'd lived alone since the end of her ill-fated marriage nine years ago. But she wasn't stupid, and she wasn't foolishly brave. Even after a few courses on self-protection, she didn't take chances.

She pulled to a stop in front of the house, carefully scanned it for any signs of life, then surveyed the surrounding meadow before finally unlocking her door and going to the back to let Bailey loose.

The dog bounded out of the cage with a joyful yip and ran in ever widening circles, sniffing the ground and raising his head to catch scents on the breeze. He sneezed at the snow falling on his nose, then rolled ecstatically and went back to his exploring.

If there'd been any interlopers—human or otherwise—nearby, he would have erupted in frenzied barking.

She whistled and he rushed back to sit at her feet, his eyes fixed on hers. "I'm sure glad you're with me," she said, leaning down to ruffle his thick, silky coat.

"Let's check out the house before it gets any darker out here."

Clicking the door locks of the SUV, she strode up the steps and across the broad porch. A bank of dark, empty windows seemed to stare back at her as she approached.

She sorted through the set of keys the lawyer had given her, until one finally worked in the stiff lock. The door opened with a screech of rusty hinges and Bailey rushed through while she patted the wall, found a panel of switches and flipped them all.

The porch and interior lights came on, revealing a large great room with a stone fireplace at one end. Ghostly white sheets were draped over lumpy, massive objects—furnishings of some sort—set about the room. A rustic, open staircase rose to a narrow balcony overlooking the first floor. Several closed doors on the second level were probably bedrooms.

Straight across the room she could see through a door to the kitchen, while to the right there appeared to be a hallway leading to the other rooms on the first floor.

Everything was covered in thick dust and the stale air was filled with the cloying odor of dead mice.

A wave of sadness hit her at everything she'd missed after the disappearance of her mother. A home of her own. Relatives. Someone to love her. Yet Thalia Rose Porter had lived here alone all those years, and only in death had she bothered to acknowledge her late nephew's daughter.

Just one more sad page among many, though dwelling on the past was useless.

Kris cautiously stepped further inside and closed the door behind her, hesitant to lock it until she knew the coast was clear.

Bailey bounced up the stairs and sniffed at the closed doors, then raced back down, his tail wagging. She released a pent-up breath as she walked to the center of the room. "Good boy."

He romped past her, sniffing at furnishings and old boxes piled in the corner—then suddenly skidded to a stop, his legs tangling in panic as he whirled to stare at the front door, barking furiously.

A coyote? A wolf, or a stray dog?

Kris heard the crunch of footsteps in the snow, moving fast.

Human. Heavy.

Another footstep, this time on the porch. She watched, mesmerized, as the doorknob turned slowly.

Her heart lodged in her throat, Kris judged the distance to the entryway, then frantically scanned the room for something. Anything that she could use as a weapon.

There was nothing.

She spun around, her heart hammering against her ribs as she tried to calculate the distance to the kitchen and a possible escape route out a back door.

A terrifying image flashed through her thoughts— a child screaming…screaming…screaming…

Oh, Laura—I still miss you so much.

But God hadn't stopped Laura's killer, so He surely wasn't going to step in now. Thinking otherwise was a waste of time.

Kris turned and started to run for the kitchen.

The front door swung open and crashed against the wall.

Over her shoulder she saw a towering figure in black fill the doorway, a rifle held against his chest. "Don't move. Don't even *think* about it, lady." His deep, gravelly voice turned harsh and low. "Unless you want more trouble than you can imagine."

She jerked to a halt. Just ten more feet and she could've made it through the kitchen door.

Growling, Bailey backpedaled, his toenails slipping and sliding against the slick hardwood floor until he managed to cower behind her legs.

"W-who are you?" she managed around the lump in her throat. "What are you doing here?"

"I could ask you the same thing," he snapped. "Since you're trespassing on private property. Now turn around—but do it *slow.*"

He took a step forward, favoring his left leg as he stepped into the light. His black Stetson cast his face in shadows, but now she could see his broad shoulders and his big, capable hands holding that rifle with an easy confidence that made the weapon seem like an extension of himself.

She had the gut-deep feeling that if he chose to shoot, he was a man who would never, ever miss.

"I—I live here, now," she explained. Her voice

sounded high and breathy, even to her own ears, and she swallowed back her fear. She slowly reached into her jacket pocket.

"Don't. Move." He snarled each distinct word.

Bailey gained courage and edged from behind her legs, his growls deepening.

"And keep your dog there, lady. Don't make me do anything we'll both regret."

Think. Think.

Turning slightly away, she reached down for the dog's collar and gripped it tightly to still her trembling fingers, easing her other hand into her pocket for her cell phone at the same time.

Pressing the "1" would speed-dial 911.

But did 911 work out here?

Was there even any reception? Surrounded by massive granite mountains and towering foothills between here and town, maybe not.

And would the local sheriff bother to follow up if she surreptitiously dialed but couldn't talk? Did he even have the capability to pinpoint this place via cellphone towers in the area?

The weight of fear and helplessness gripped her stomach in a painful knot. Despite the cold, sweat trickled down her back.

If he took a single step toward her, she would spin around and run for her life—and risk the chance that she could get the back door open in time. With luck, she could even make it to the SUV—

The intruder pushed back one side of his full-length

Australian outback coat and unclipped his own cell from his belt. Without taking his eyes from her face, he hit a single speed-dial button, then held the phone to his ear.

"Yep—this is Trace, Sheriff…"

His words stunned her, filled her with sudden hope.

"…and I need you out here right away. I just caught another one of those vandals, and you won't want to let this one get away."

Trace Randall scowled at the woman as he snapped his phone shut.

He'd seen the dark SUV slow down far ahead of his truck, as if the driver was searching for an easy mark. When it turned up the road to the old Porter place, he'd known his instincts were right.

Thalia had been gone for over a year. Six months ago he'd discovered a wild drunken group of teens partying in her barn, and thieves had broken into the cabin just last month, though he and his cowhands had scared them all off before they'd had a chance to do much damage. Set so far back from the road, the place was an attractive lure to those who wanted to avoid watchful eyes. He'd known it would only be a matter of time before trouble struck again.

That anyone would come out here, under cover of approaching darkness, to steal dear old Thalia's possessions gave him a serious case of heartburn.

But that the thief was a young woman this time flat-out surprised him. Though she was bundled up in a heavy coat, her hair hidden in a stocking cap, she didn't look like she was more than thirty—if that.

And though her face was chalk-white at being caught in the act, she looked halfway attractive. What was this world coming to?

"Y-you called the sheriff? Really?" she whispered.

The note of hope in her voice made him pause. "You heard me. He's sending out a deputy, and fortunately the guy isn't too far away."

Her shoulders sagged with obvious relief, and she reached up to pull off her stocking cap. A cascade of sun-streaked blond curls rippled across her shoulders like warm honey. "Well," she said with a sigh, "if that's the truth, I can't tell you how glad I am to hear it."

Despite her casual words, she took a cautious step back, and then another.

"I wouldn't try to leave, if I were you."

"It's you who'll be leaving once that deputy gets here." She leaned down and murmured something to the dog, then released her hold on its collar. The dog sat at her side, its eyes riveted on Trace. "This place belongs to me now. I've got the attorney's letter about the inheritance in my truck."

He narrowed his eyes. "Which attorney? From where?"

"Carl Baxter. He has a satellite office in Battle Creek. I met with him at his main office though… down in Lost Falls."

Anyone could have had that information ready as a cover.

"He was Thalia Porter's attorney," she added. "He handled her will."

"How long ago did she die?"

The woman lifted a shoulder. "January of last year, I guess. I never met her. I only heard about it a few months ago."

Her story sounded more implausible by the minute. Trace glanced at his watch, wishing the deputy would hurry up. There were cattle to feed and horses to bring up from the pasture back at the ranch. And if he was lucky, there might even be a hot supper warming in the oven if his sister, Carrie, had gotten back from Billings.

"So you never met Ms. Porter and didn't know she'd died. Yet she left you her property?"

"Strange, I know. Supposedly she was my great-aunt, so surely she must have known about me. I keep wondering why she never bothered to track me down. I was left in foster care from the age of ten, and I guess now it's too late for any answers." A thread of anger and hurt simmered in her voice. "Until recently I didn't even know she existed. Go ahead—search my truck and find that paper. And while you're at it, check out everything else in there. If you think you're going to find stolen goods, you'll be sadly mistaken."

From outside came the sound of tires crunching through the snow, and Trace rocked back on his heels and smiled. "I guess we'll find out pretty soon. And if any part of your story isn't true, I imagine you'll be seeing the inside of the Latimer County Jail."

TWO

The deputy—Ken Gardner, according to his name pin—shouldered his bulk through the entryway and gave the tall cowboy a clap on the back. "Got yourself a tough one, eh?"

"Not so tough—just ticked off." Kris gave the cowboy a cool glance, then shifted her attention back to the newcomer. "I imagine you've already run my plates by now and know who I am, right?"

"Ms. Kristine Donaldson, from Boise. No criminal record that I could find. So what are you doing out here all alone?"

"Like I told this guy, I'm Thalia Porter's great-niece…or was. Her lawyer tracked me down."

The deputy pursed his lips. "She lived out here a good ten years, and we were on some county-fair committees together, every year. Never did hear her mention any kin—in fact, more 'n once she talked about not having any left."

"Well, I must be the last living relative Baxter could

find if he had to settle on me." Kris felt her heartbeat stumble at the thought of her sister, who had dropped from sight so many years ago. The lawyer, apparently, hadn't located Emma. Who knew if she was even still alive? "Thalia was my dad's aunt, but he died when I was three. My mother wouldn't have anything to do with his family after that."

"I suppose you have some sort of proof of all this?"

"In my glove box." She pulled her keys from her pocket and tossed them over to him. "Be my guest."

The deputy nodded and went out the front door, leaving the cowboy behind.

He still cradled the rifle across his chest, and though his John Wayne intensity had faded, he was still a formidable man. She was suddenly very, very glad that he seemed to be on the right side of the law.

"Assuming Ken finds what he's looking for, I'm curious," he drawled. "What would possess a woman to come clear out here this late, alone?"

"That old strip motel in town was the only lodging place open. It didn't look at all promising from the outside, so I kept going." She lifted her chin. "Who are you, anyway?"

He took another step into the room and took off his hat. "Trace Randall. I own the ranch next door."

He'd seemed dangerous before, but now she felt her stomach do a shaky little tap dance for an entirely different reason.

A rakish lock of rich black hair tumbled over his high forehead, and laugh lines crinkled at the corners of his warm brown eyes—probably more from a lifetime spent in the Montana sun than from good humor, given his scowl, but attractive nonetheless.

From his rugged, square jaw and strong, high cheekbones to that straight blade of a nose, he looked more like someone who ought to be in the movies than a real-life cowboy standing in front of her wearing faded jeans and well-worn boots.

But for all that, he was exactly the kind of man she always took great care to avoid, thanks to Allan's enduring legacy of disillusionment and heartbreak.

Firmly shoving the memories of her ex-husband into the past, she met the rancher's steady gaze with one of her own. "Quite a welcoming committee," she said coolly. "I can hardly wait to meet the rest of the neighbors."

"Not many out here. The Rocking R ranch is to the north, and Bureau of Land Management grazing land borders the other three sides of Thalia's property. The ranch holding the BLM lease is a good forty miles away."

"The Rocking R is yours?"

He nodded.

The deputy stomped across the porch and came inside, dusting a sparkling shawl of snow from his shoulders. "Guess we owe you an apology, ma'am." He stepped forward, his hand extended. "Welcome to Battle Creek."

She accepted the brief handshake, then glanced at Trace. "I suppose I should thank you for keeping watch over this place. It's been empty for what—almost a year?"

"Thereabouts." Gardner tipped his head toward the rear entrance. "An empty, isolated place like this one spells trouble, once word gets out, but Trace has been keeping an eye on things. Six months ago, he discovered a drunken group of teens out here, and he recently interrupted a break-in."

Kris suppressed an inward shudder. "It must have been a good feeling to catch all of them."

"We nabbed some of the teens, but the thieves got away. I doubt they'd be stupid enough to come back, though."

Or they could figure that the law would think exactly that, and brazenly return. "I hope that's true."

The deputy grinned at Trace. "You've got a real good man next door, ma'am, if you get yourself all scared, bein' here alone."

The patronizing good-old-boy camaraderie between the two men sent her blood into a slow simmer. "Thanks, but I doubt that'll happen. I can take care of myself."

Trace searched her face. "Like you did when I showed up?" he asked, his voice gentle. "Take care, ma'am. This isn't exactly the suburbs out here. Even the locals respect the mountains…and what they can hide."

Long after the deputy and Trace left, the rancher's words played through Kris's thoughts, and the chill she felt the next morning had nothing to do with the balky furnace and a lying thermostat that claimed the temperature had risen to eighty-two.

She'd grown up in this part of Montana, more or less, depending on her current foster family.

She knew about the rapid and dangerous changes in weather up here. The lightning storms that could pop up out of nowhere at the higher elevations. The way a stream trickling down a mountain could become a roaring, terrifying flood come the spring melt.

And she knew all too well about what the dense forests and wild, rocky terrain could hide. Bears and wolves, but also two-legged creatures who could be the most frightening of all.

Ruthless killers who could torture and kill a young, innocent girl like her friend Laura. Drug runners coming across the mountains from California and Mexico, who would stop at nothing to protect their illicit trade.

Even a mother, who could walk away from her daughters without a backward glance, and never return.

Kris and Emma had seen her leave that evening, and for years they'd had terrifying nightmares about her being eaten by the bears or wolves in the forest. With age came the jaded realization that she'd probably slipped away to run off with a boyfriend, without any regard for the two little girls she'd left behind…alone, in an empty apartment.

Kris had dealt with it all before she turned twenty-one, and she no longer wasted time on any foolish mis-conceptions about the inherent goodness in people.

Kneeling, she murmured to Bailey. The old dog lumbered to his feet and came over to rest his head on her shoulder. "We're going to make a go of this, aren't we? Then come spring, we'll sell out and be on our way."

He wagged his tail against the floor, sweeping an arc in the thick dust.

She grinned. "And I can see you'll be a lot of help, too."

He wiggled against her, trying to crawl into her lap just as he had as a pup, and they both fell over in a heap. She laughed as she ruffled the thick fur on his neck.

The dog suddenly stiffened and stared at the door. Gave one low bark. Then he bounded over to the entryway and clawed at the door, his tail wagging furiously.

So it was probably somebody he'd met, like Trace—proving there was no accounting for taste—or maybe even the deputy.

Still, Kris peered out a window first and, seeing a black pickup with Rocking R emblazoned on the side, she sighed.

But it wasn't Trace scowling at her when she opened the heavy oak door. It was a petite woman who might have been his clone, given her dark, wavy hair and flashing brown eyes, except for the fact that she had the megawatt grin of an enchanting pixie.

"Hi there!" she chirped, lifting a bulky cardboard box high for inspection. "I have a feeling my brother wasn't exactly friendly, so I'm here to repair the damage. I'm his sister, Carrie, by the way. I live in one of the cabins over at his place." Her smile dimmed a few watts. "At least for now."

"Come on in." Kris unhooked the screen door and pushed it wide open to usher her inside.

Carrie headed straight for the kitchen and plopped the box on the counter. "Whew. Hope you don't mind me making myself at home," she said over her shoulder as she pulled out loaves of homemade bread, bags of cookies and finally a casserole dish that she slipped into the refrigerator. "This box was heavier than I thought."

No wonder Bailey had been excited at the woman's approach. "It all smells wonderful." Kris inhaled the wonderful aromas. "What is it?"

"Lasagna. Homemade garlic-and-herb bread. My version of chocolate-chip cookies—loaded with white chocolate, dried cranberries and pecans." She laughed. "Trace says I'm obsessed with drowning my sorrows in food. Really, I just like to cook, and there's only him and me now, since the hands are both married."

Kris surreptitiously glanced at her bare left hand.

Carrie turned and leaned against the counter, her dimples deepening. "Yeah, I'm single. Billy walked out six months ago, and I should be thankful it's over. But life sure throws us some curves sometimes, doesn't it?"

If she only knew. "I—I'm sorry."

"Thanks, but don't be. I'm a 'till death do us part' kind of gal, and he was a 'till I'm out of sight' kinda guy." She shook her head slowly and sighed. "When Trace found out, it was all I could do to keep him from taking Billy apart, piece by piece, though some folks thought Billy had it coming."

Bemused by the flood of personal revelations from a complete stranger, Kris could only try for a comforting smile in return.

"Over, done with." Carrie flapped her hands with a dismissive air. "So how about you? Are you excited over moving here?"

"I'm just glad the trip here is over. Want some coffee to go with those cookies?" When Carrie nodded, Kris started making a pot. "The lawyer said this place needed work, but that he could simply contact a Realtor and save me the trouble if I wanted to sell."

Carrie's mouth dropped open. "You'd really *sell* this place?"

Kris nodded. "I figure this is my one chance to…" She hesitated. "Well, to make some dreams come true. I hope to fix it up a little, so it can bring a better price."

Carrie gave her an odd look. "You got here last night, right? Have you walked the property in the daylight yet? Taken a really good look?"

"Nope. I started making my project list for inside the house, though. *Sweat equity* has taken on a whole lot more meaning now that I see how much has to be done."

Carrie reached for the bag of cookies, pulled a paper plate from a package Kris had left on the counter and shook a few cookies onto the plate. Bailey immediately took up his silent I'm-a-starving-orphan position at her feet and looked up at her with adoring eyes. On the counter, the coffeemaker gurgled and spat.

"I guess you didn't know Thalia," Carrie murmured after she polished off a cookie.

"Never met her. I wish I had—it would've been nice just knowing that I had a relative somewhere."

Even after all these years, a hint of wistfulness must have crept into her voice, because Carrie looked up sharply. "You had *no* one?"

Apparently Trace wasn't a gossipy sort of guy. "I told your brother about it. I was raised in the area, but my dad died when I was young, and my mom split a few years later. I grew up in foster homes, mostly. I have a sister somewhere, but haven't seen her in years."

Carrie's expressive face crumpled with sympathy. "I'm so, so sorry."

Kris shrugged and turned to pour a couple of cups of coffee, then slid the carafe back into the coffeemaker so it could finish the rest of its brewing cycle.

She handed Carrie a cup, and cradled the other between her palms, savoring the warmth. "So what was Thalia like?"

"She loved this place so much. She raised golden

retrievers and had a whole army of cats in the barn, along with a couple horses and a pet cow."

"A pet *cow?*"

"It started out as an injured calf that she rescued after it wandered onto her property. She insisted on paying Trace for it, then she could never bear to let it go back to a herd. She eventually established a private no-kill shelter of sorts here." Carrie's eyes lit with obvious fondness. "She loved hiking up into the mountains to paint nature scenes, which she sold at some of the tourist shops in town. She played classical music on her piano. She was my piano teacher when I was a teen."

"Sounds like a pretty interesting lady."

"She was." Carrie laughed lightly. "You could sure see her coming. She wore brilliantly colored caftans with lots of silver jewelry, and she had the reddest hair I ever saw. I…I still can't believe she's gone. She was only sixty when she fell to her death. She would've loved meeting you," Carrie added softly. "She once told me how she enjoyed teaching her piano students because she'd never married or had kids of her own. Even with all her pets, I imagine she was lonely sometimes."

Until now, Thalia Porter had been only a name on some documents. A shadowy figure who had never bothered to track down a hurting child, lost in the foster care system for too many years. But now a sense of longing and loss filled Kris's heart for the first time at the thought of the fascinating woman she would never get to meet.

"She fell in some sort of ravine up in the mountains, right? That's what the lawyer said."

Carrie nodded. "She was on a trail she'd hiked countless times, heading for one of her favorite vistas to paint. She died doing what she enjoyed most."

"It's a shame she died so young, though."

Carrie took a sip of coffee and looked pensively out the front window of the cabin to the faint silhouette of the mountains cloaked in a thick morning haze. "Everyone around here loved her, and I miss her terribly, but I guess none of us know when our time will be up. We just need to do our best to live a good and loving life, keep our faith in God and not do anything we'll regret."

Regret. Something Kris had lived with for a long, long time. She murmured vague words of agreement as she turned away to fiddle with the coffeepot.

Things hadn't been easy for Carrie, either, yet the young woman still seemed to glow with happiness and contentment. What would it be like to feel that confident, that positive about her faith and about what life promised?

If only I'd made the right decisions years ago...

But even now, she knew that her past would be catching up to her. There'd be a phone call...or a letter. It would start all over again.

And she'd long ago given up on praying for a reprieve.

THREE

Carrie's words played through Kris's thoughts as she followed her out to the Rocking R truck parked outside.

"So what do you think?" Carrie stopped at the driver's-side door and gave Kris an expectant look. "Dinner tomorrow night around seven? Just go four miles north and look for the Rocking R sign on the left. Can't miss it."

Jerked back to the present, Kris gave her an embarrassed smile and wondered what else she'd missed in Carrie's mile-a-minute conversation. "I…well…"

"Nothing fancy, believe me." Carrie opened the door and grinned. "After working on this place all day, a hot meal ought to feel good. It'll probably be just the two of us, though."

No surprise, there. "I get the feeling that Trace isn't exactly happy to have me move in next door."

Carrie snorted. "He isn't exactly Mr. Sociable, is he? But…he has his reasons. He's actually a great guy—once you get to know him."

"I'm sorry. I didn't mean…"

"No, I understand. But he didn't dream up an excuse to be gone, or anything. He's got some people coming to look at horses tomorrow afternoon and after that he has a fire investigation the other end of the county."

"He's in insurance, too?"

"No." She lifted a shoulder. "He's been with the volunteer fire department most of his adult life, so when the county's on-call arson investigator retired a couple years ago, Trace was asked if he'd take the necessary classes and certification to replace him." She chuckled. "He took something like fifteen seminars, and even had to travel out of state for some of them. But one thing about Trace—he's the go-to guy for anything that comes his way, and he's definitely not a quitter."

"I…guess not," Kris murmured. His sister clearly loved him, but the news of his planned absence made the invitation all the more appealing.

Carrie's forehead puckered. "Oh—I forgot to tell you. He was over early this morning and moved that downed tree blocking your road. He's sending one of the men over with a chain saw later on, so you'll have a good stack of firewood out of it."

Surprised at his thoughtfulness, Kris murmured her thanks, then watched Carrie's pickup rumble across the snowy meadow and out of sight around a curve leading into the trees.

Bailey bounded through the drifts to her side, his

tongue lolling and his wagging tail sending up a cloud of snow.

"Let's go check everything out, okay?"

He loped around her in circles as she started for the buildings behind the house. Set against the backdrop of a solid wall of pines rimming the clearing, both structures were weathered to pale silver. One was long and low, maybe thirty by sixty, with what appeared to be an office and entry jutting out from the center.

The other building was a small, traditional hip-roofed barn, where Thalia had probably kept her little herd of livestock safe and warm.

Bailey scratched at the door of the kennel building, so Kris started there first, trying different keys on her ring until the door finally opened.

Inside, a massive desk and multiple file cabinets filled the right wall, though most of the space was devoted to what appeared to be a pet-grooming and veterinary-exam area, with a stainless-steel exam table, washtubs and glass-fronted supply cupboards.

Nice facilities, except the area was filled to the ceiling with junk of all kinds—old mowers, sagging, damp cardboard boxes, wooden crates of moldering books.

The next door led to the kennel area, where an aisle stretched to the left and right, flanked with dog pens on both sides. A series of skylights filtered dim light into the interior, revealing piles of old furniture. Bedsprings. Rusted barrels. Stacks of yellowed newspapers and more magazines.

Something skittered through the shadows and Bailey lunged after it, barking madly until he reached the end of the building and skidded to a confused halt. Whining, he scrabbled at a moldering tower of cardboard boxes, though why he thought any rodent would stick around amidst the din was anybody's guess.

Kris wrapped her arms around her middle and rubbed her upper arms to stimulate the circulation as she walked the length of the building to the left and then the right, her breath visible in steamy puffs.

Clearly there hadn't been an estate auction after Thalia's death, and these jumbled piles of possessions were all that was left of her life.

The sadness of it all nearly robbed Kris of breath as she turned slowly and took it in.

This had once been a nice kennel, she realized.

The pens were spacious, constructed of ten-foot-high chain-link panels. Through the few pens that weren't filled with junk, she could see dog doors leading outside to what must have been individual exercise runs flanking the full length of the building on both the front and back, though those facing the cabin were gone and the ones at the rear had been reduced to a tumbledown mess.

Pools of ice glittered like miniature skating rinks under places where the roof probably leaked. It was musty and cold and dreary, probably a haven for untold numbers of mice…or worse.

Just sorting and moving out all of this stuff would take more work than she could imagine. And the repairs…

Not only did the house need a lot of work, but the outbuildings did, too, if the place was to be listed at a good price.

And just like that, Kris's dreams of sprucing the place up for a quick sale dissipated.

"Helloooo—are you out here?" Carrie's familiar voice drifted through one of the broken windows.

Kris whistled to Bailey and opened the door. "Over here," she called. "In the kennel."

The sun had broken free of the clouds while she'd been inside, and now she blinked at the blinding glare of the snow. As her eyes adjusted, she drew in a sharp breath at the stunning vista in front of her.

Last night it had been too dark to see anything, and until now low-lying clouds had obliterated the view.

Massive, snow-capped granite peaks soared sky-ward, filling the entire western horizon, too stunning, too beautiful to be real. With the curve of the meadow, it was as if they were close enough to touch—so breathtaking that she couldn't look away.

Awe enveloped her, leaving her speechless and dazed.

"I realized that I didn't have your cell number, so I came back to give you this." Carrie rounded the corner of the barn, a piece of paper fluttering in her hand. "It's the name of a Realtor I know, and—"

She pulled to a stop a few yards away, a knowing smile on her lips. "Ahh. You've seen the view."

Kris nodded silently, unable to break the spell that enfolded her.

Carrie turned to face the Rockies and backed up slowly until she reached Kris's side. "This spot has the most perfect view of any place I know," she murmured. "I think Thalia must've painted it a hundred times, but said she never tired of it. She thought every season and every moment of the day had its own unique beauty—like God was painting His own incredible picture each time."

"There are no words," Kris whispered.

Carrie offered the sheet of paper. "Karen is a seasoned Realtor. She's done a lot of the multimillion-dollar resorts, but some of the small properties, as well. I called her on my cell a few minutes ago and told her about you. She said real estate is really tough right now, and that a lot of places are staying on the market for a year or more. But she can give it a try if you just want to get rid of the place."

The words sounded raw, almost blasphemous. As jarring as the screech of chalk on a blackboard. "Get…rid of it?" Kris said faintly.

"You did say you wanted to sell out so you could do something else, didn't you?"

"I…I guess." Kris shook her head to clear her thoughts. "My ex-husband had quite a bit of legal trouble, and he ran us into a lot of debt—in my name as well as his. I've struggled ever since, with trying to pay off that, plus my college loans."

And she'd spent even more on private investigators while trying to find Emma, though she tried not to dwell on that. One false lead after another had finally ended with no leads at all…though she was still paying a monthly bill from the last investigator she'd hired.

Carrie gave her a sympathetic smile. "Bad situation."

"I figured I could clean this place up a little and sell it, clear all of my debts and finally go back to college." She sighed. "But it's going to take a lot more time and money than I thought. I've only got a few thousand dollars in savings."

"So why doesn't your ex chip in on those debts?"

"He isn't responsible enough to feed a goldfish, and my name was on those papers, too. I don't even know where he is from one month to the next. *Unless* he calls begging for 'a little loan.' I did that once years ago and never again, but he still doesn't quite get it. He somehow figures I 'owe' him."

Carrie nodded with complete understanding. "I've been there, believe me. So what would you major in if you got this place sold?"

"Vet school." Kris managed a rueful smile. "I muddled around with different majors for way too long, and a pile of liberal arts credits with a lot of debt and no degree isn't a particularly good career path. I finally went back to school and became a vet tech, so I could actually find a job."

Carrie pursed her lips. "How did you like that?"

"I worked at a large clinic and volunteered at a shelter on weekends." Kris shrugged. "I loved it, but now I want to do even more. I'm fascinated with medicine and surgery."

"So you need money to fix this place up, and it's going to take time."

"Too much, on both counts." Kris sighed. "I suppose I should just list it as is, but after seeing this view, I hate the thought of selling it below market just because I didn't take the time to clean it up."

"There was an article in our little local paper, just last week. I wonder if you'd be interested." Carrie trotted back to her pickup and foraged through a box of papers on the backseat. "I probably have it with the other recyclables, right here."

Kris followed her and watched as she searched to the bottom of the box, then carefully rechecked each magazine and newspaper as she put them all back.

"Voilà!" She cried, holding a thin newspaper aloft. "Read this, and see what you think."

Kris accepted the *Battle Creek Courier* and scanned the front page, then the second. On the third, a photo of a forlorn dog caught her eye. "This article, about the dog?"

"Read it!" Carrie's eyes lit with excitement. "The county closed the humane shelter last fall because they didn't have enough funding to maintain the old building and keep it running. But now they have to send strays clear over to the next county and pay boarding fees on them, plus all the transportation costs. Some of our local residents are irate over the whole deal, saying it's a waste of taxpayers' money."

Kris scanned the article. "Do they want to build another facility, then?"

"I guess so." Carrie peered over her shoulder at the paper. "I don't see the details here, but apparently it'll take at least a year for planning and fundraising. In the meantime, the county wants to temporarily hire someone with a kennel to operate a privately run shelter for them." She waved expansively, her gesture encompassing the outbuildings and the entire meadow. "I understand there'd be a flat monthly salary plus daily fees paid for each animal being housed."

"Y-you're thinking *this* place would work?"

"You've got room for every kind of livestock here, as well as pets. You could use your salary for fixing the place up, then sell it later on."

Kris felt an ember of excitement flicker to life, then fade as she surveyed the property. "But this place is a mess. By the time I get it up to code for a shelter, someone else could nab the opportunity. I'd just end up deeper in debt."

"Call the county at least, and find out if they've had any nibbles. Maybe you could even apply for a provisional contract. I do happen to know some of the powers-that-be down at the courthouse," Carrie added with a grin. "Maybe I can find out for you."

Kris felt that ember of excitement come to life again. "It wouldn't hurt to try, I guess."

"Exactly. I can't even imagine what this place will be worth once it's back in shape." Carrie gave her a quick hug. "Come to think of it, Trace is an old friend of the woman who managed the previous shelter, so I can make sure he introduces you. I'll bet she'd be a good source of information."

The possibility that Carrie's brother might be willing to help Kris with *anything* seemed beyond comprehension, but what would it hurt to try?

Trace called an hour after Carrie left to ask if Kris could meet him in town at eleven, proving that Carrie was definitely a force to be reckoned with—even with her cool, distant brother.

Kris arrived a few minutes early and found him leaning against the hood of his pickup in front of the Polly's Dandy Darlings pet salon.

Even from a distance, she'd recognized his lean, chiseled profile beneath the brim of his black Stetson and the way his waist-length black down jacket accented the breadth of his shoulders and those narrow hips.

If the silly flutter in her midsection was any indication, someone needed to hire the man for a Levi's jeans commercial…or put him astride a horse on the silver screen as the epitome of a lean, laconic cowboy.

He turned as she approached, a faint, lazy smile briefly touching the corners of his mouth. "You and my sister definitely operate on different schedules."

"Oh?" She glanced at her watch. "Am I late?"

His smile kicked up a notch. "You're on time."

The glimpse of his humor sent her flutters into overdrive. "Well, it's a rare thing for me, too."

He motioned toward the shop. "After you."

She nodded and walked through the door he held open for her. Inside, a tall, rawboned woman, with silver hair twisted into a knot atop her head, looked up from unpacking a box of merchandise on the counter.

Trace sauntered into the store. "Kris Donaldson, I'd like you to meet Polly Norcross. Polly managed the Battle Creek humane shelter for years."

"Until it went under." Polly's voice was filled with regret. "I just wish things had been different."

"Polly did a wonderful job." Trace moved to the counter and leaned against it on one elbow. "But there were a number of shortfalls in the county budget, and then the local economy took a dive when gas prices fluctuated and tourism took a hit."

"True. That last year, we struggled just to keep going. By the end we couldn't even cover the only two salaried positions, and the two of us were paying for dog food out of our own savings. Luckily, I had this business to fall back on, or I probably would've had to leave the area." Polly nodded at Kris. "I hear you're thinking about running the shelter."

"I am, but I could sure use more information and some advice. Do you have a minute?"

Polly laughed at that. "An hour or two is more like it. As you can see, it's not a busy day."

"I hear this is just an interim contract. How temporary do you think it will be?"

Polly snorted. "Latimer County's animal control has been in a mess since our facility closed. The fools on the county board let our own buildings fall to ruin and we lost the entire infrastructure that made our system work so well. Now, they're talking about raising funds and starting all over with a new building. There'll be feasibility studies, research on locations, architects, construction bids. They figure on a year or so, max. I'm guessing that's incredibly optimistic."

"So the private contract could end up running longer."

"Definitely. With a nice, central location like Thalia's place, they might even see the benefit of just continuing to contract with a private kennel—though that's just a guess." She sniffed in disdain. "They don't always follow the soundest logic."

"Is the policy-and-procedure manual still available from when you were the manager?"

Surprise flared in Polly's eyes. "There've been a few folks interested in winning the shelter contract, but you're the first one who asked about the old policies."

"I figure there's more to opening a shelter than just the state and local regulations. I hear you ran a tight ship."

"All of the records are in boxes somewhere in the basement of the courthouse. But I did keep a copy of that manual, just in case any questions arose. I could run off an extra copy for you if you'd like to see how things were done."

"That would be fantastic."

"Running a shelter isn't just about picking up

strays, or welcoming loving families who are begging to adopt cute puppies and kittens." Polly eyed her closely. "We held puppy training classes and workshops, and offered a variety of events. Over time, we developed quite a roster of volunteers, too. The local vets were good about working with us, so that's a relationship you'd need to rebuild. And…not every citizen is pleasant. Working with the public can be difficult."

"I worked as a vet tech back home. I also volunteered for the past year at a no-kill shelter. I do know the realities…though of course the management side will be something new."

Polly braced her palms on the counter top and gave Kris another long, assessing look, then nodded at Trace. "She'll do."

He cracked another brief smile. "Carrie is certainly convinced."

"There'll be a lot of work to do before I can even take the next step, though." Kris fingered her ring of keys, as her doubt started to grow. "It'll take a lot of time."

"Go for it. We *need* a shelter in this county, and we need it soon," Polly retorted. "If you get the job, I'll see what I can do about helping you out, and maybe I can rally the old volunteers. For another thing, the shelter's rescue truck is parked out behind the courthouse, and some of the cages are out at one of the county highway department sheds. If the board doesn't offer that equipment to you, come talk to me."

"You might have a little extra help before that, too," Trace said, his eyes twinkling.

Twinkling? Surprised at the flash of warmth in his expression, Kris stared up at him. "Really?"

"Carrie wants to help you out in every way she can." He laughed in a low and affectionate way that conveyed their close relationship. "She's already let me know that I'll be coming over to help you out as soon as I can—and so will my hired men. Believe me—no one stands in her way for long."

Trace shoved his hands in his back pockets and stared out the window of Polly's store after Kris left, feeling as if he'd been run over by a truck. Carrie's truck, to be exact. With all hundred and ten pounds of her in it…and maybe a Brahma in the back.

For the past five years he'd been alone, and he'd carefully made sure things stayed that way. Yet twenty minutes with Kris and he felt like some teenage boy longing after the prom queen he'd never have. Had he actually flirted with her? *Flirted?*

"You look a little stunned." Polly gave a low laugh. "Did this new neighbor of yours turn out a tad different than you'd expected?"

"I wasn't even *expecting* a new neighbor." He offered Polly a rueful smile. "The first time we met, I thought she was a prowler and tried to get her arrested."

"Really slick, Trace." Polly's eyebrows lifted in amusement. "Let me guess—Carrie came riding to the rescue, took Kris's side and now she's having you make amends?"

He tipped his head in acknowledgment. "But I oughta help her out, anyhow. That's what neighbors do up here, and she's a woman alone."

"Well, she's sure a nice gal," Polly teased. "Pretty, too. Maybe you'd better start paying closer attention, or the other guys around here will nab her first."

Trace felt a cold fist tighten around his heart. "Just as well."

Polly silently studied him, then shrugged and went back to unpacking the box of merchandise. "Your loss, their gain, I guess."

It was a conversation he didn't want to continue. Snagging his truck keys from his jacket pocket, he headed for the door. "Thanks for talking to her, Polly. I owe you."

On the way back to the ranch, he tried to concentrate on the calves he had to vaccinate today and the horses he needed to work. But instead his thoughts kept straying to his new neighbor.

Polly was right about her, no doubt about that.

Kris's gleaming, honey-gold hair made him want to touch it, just to see if it was as silky as it looked. Her delicate features made him wish he could please her, just to see her smile, though her obvious independence, courage and straightforward manner were what attracted him the most.

But there was no way he was going to pursue a closer relationship with her or anyone else.

Except for Carrie, no one here knew about what had happened while he'd been away on the rodeo circuit a few years back. A double nightmare—a friend's terrible rodeo accident that Trace could've prevented, and a betrayal by another friend that haunted him still. He never wanted to risk that kind of heartbreak again.

Developing a plan was one thing. Implementing it was another.

After spending the rest of the day researching building codes and state regulations on shelter facilities, and contacting the county about her plans, Kris scheduled a preliminary inspection on Monday, then buckled down to work.

On Wednesday morning she found a rusted trailer behind the kennel, hooked it to her SUV and began filling it with trash from inside the pens.

But after taking four loads to the landfill by noon, she wearily dropped onto a wobbly bench by the door to the office.

Bailey rose awkwardly from the bed of folded blankets next to the bench and came to rest his head on her lap, his wise old eyes searching her face.

"What have we gotten ourselves into, buddy?" she whispered to him, leaning down to give him a hug. "Five hours, and I can't even see any difference."

At a sharp rap on the door at the end of the aisle, she startled, but Bailey just wagged his tail and woofed. The door squealed open and Trace filled the doorway, brushing the snow off his shoulders.

He flashed a quick grin. "Carrie tells me you need help today."

Surprised, she straightened and dusted off her hands, trying to ignore the sudden tingle of nerves dancing in her midsection at his arrival. "I didn't really expect you to pitch in. I mean…you must have a lot to do at your own place."

He sauntered down the long aisle and stood before her, a good six feet of casual male grace dressed in faded jeans and a leather jacket cut trim at his narrow waist.

He hooked a thumb in a front pocket and swept his hat off with his other hand. "Well, ma'am, if I don't follow through, Carrie won't be happy—and then she probably won't fix me dinner." The long dimples bracketing his mouth deepened. "And dinner is something I surely hate to miss."

He took a long, measuring glance down the aisle to the mountains of boxes and old furnishings still filling most of the dog pens. "All this stuff has to go?"

"I wish it were that easy." Kris glanced down the aisle and sighed. "Some of it, yes—the mice have had a field day with the linens and such. But still, there are some treasures mixed in with the trash."

"Treasures?"

"Of sorts." She dredged up a smile. "Did you know my aunt very well?"

"Thalia was my neighbor, but also a friend. She was one of the more interesting gals in town, honestly. A real free spirit and as straightforward as they come."

"I just wish I'd met her. I didn't even know she existed until after she was gone. And from some of the things I've been finding here, I think I would have enjoyed her so much."

He nodded. "I sure did. If you ever wanted an honest opinion about anything, you didn't need to go any farther than Thalia's front door."

"I can imagine." Kris laughed.

"And she definitely wasn't just a Sunday Christian. She lived her faith by helping anyone who needed help, no matter who they were…but she wasn't looking for recognition or thanks." His mouth lifted into a wry grin. "She was the kind of gal who made you wish your own faith was a whole lot stronger."

Since starting to go through Thalia's things in the kennel, Kris had felt an empty place in her heart start to grow. Now it expanded even more. What would it be like to be so secure in your faith?

Kris truly did believe in God. She just wasn't too sure that He cared a lot about her. If He hadn't protected Laura all those years ago, as sweet as she'd been, what were the chances that He was going to carefully watch over someone like Kris—much less forgive her for what she'd done?

She'd tried not to dwell on it. She'd worked hard to live a good life since. But nothing could ever erase her past, and it was all still there for anyone to find, back in her legal records. A time bomb, just waiting to go off.

"Quite a few things need to go to the landfill, and

some boxes I'll be taking to Goodwill. But there are so many interesting books and mementos from her travels—not to mention all of her art supplies and her beautiful pottery and paintings. I can't believe it was all thrown in boxes and hauled out here for storage."

Trace frowned. "For a while, everyone assumed there were no relatives. The lawyer probably hired someone to clear out the house, to get ready for an auction."

"It's so sad, to think of Thalia's life almost being erased by the sale of her property, with no one left to treasure her memory."

"Until you were found," Trace said with a smile. "But she wasn't just the sum of her possessions. Memorial contributions in her name were used to re-furbish the library down at the community church, and for buying new hymnals. And I know people will long remember all of her efforts with the county fair and beautification projects in town. There was mention in the local paper about naming one of the fairground buildings after her, in recognition of all of the fundraising she did."

"Thank you," Kris said quietly. "I felt so discon-nected here, looking at a stranger's things and trying to make sense of it all. I'm glad to know a little bit more about my aunt. You've helped make her seem more real to me."

"So," he said, his gaze flicking from one end of the building to the other, "tell me what you want me to do. Can I help you haul anything to the landfill?"

Clearly, the moment for friendly conversation was over, and now it was time to get down to business…or else. "The dog pens have numbered signs at the top of each gate. I've been putting the trash in ten and eleven, and the boxes that'll go to the cabin are in thirteen. But really, you don't need to—"

A frown flickered across his expression. "But this is why I came."

He strode down to pick up a load of crumbling cardboard boxes, took them outside, then returned for another load. She tagged along, carrying out one load after another, until the trailer was filled once again.

"Whew," she said, as she shoved a final box in place. "I think this does it."

Trace tipped his head towards his crew cab pickup. "Let's keep going. We can put a good-size load in the back of my pickup and just tie it all down. I've got some rope."

"But then you'd have to go along to the county landfill," she protested. "That takes quite a while, and you've already done so much. You saved me at least a half a day with all you've been carrying—and you took the time to introduce me to Polly, too."

"I consider this a last favor for Thalia," he said. "She'd like to know her home was going to be taken care of and that someone would love it just as she did."

Kris felt a flash of guilt. Was that why he seemed so brusque today, as if he'd already decided Kris would be a quitter—a traitor to the memory of an aunt she'd never even met?

He turned on his heel and silently went back into the building, then returned with a stack of two boxes in his arms. With a shrug, Kris followed suit.

No matter what Trace thought of her, she was still thankful for his help. Though, between having Carrie here or her handsome, distant brother, Carrie was definitely the more enjoyable of the two.

Seeing progress lifted Kris's spirits. The ring of her cell phone a few minutes after Trace left—then reading the caller's name on the screen—splintered her optimism into shards at her feet.

"Hey, babe."

The wheedling tone made her skin crawl. She closed her eyes. "Allan. How did you get my new cell number?"

"What? You didn't think I would—especially since you've had such good luck?" His voice lowered to a seductive purr. "You must be sitting pretty, now that you own a fancy place in the mountains."

She opened her eyes again and surveyed the shabby buildings; the piles of refuse beside the kennel. "Not fancy. Run-down. Very, very run-down."

"But it just landed in your lap, didn't it? The windfall we always dreamed about. Easy street. That property must be worth *millions* up there. We can finally make a real go of being together."

Her stomach turned. "*We* never had dreams like that. You're the one who wanted to be handed life on a silver platter. And that's how you ended up in jail."

"I ended up in jail because of you, and then you had the gall to dump me while I was in there. A good wife doesn't do that." His voice snapped across the miles like a whiplash, still carrying his old anger. He'd been controlling during their marriage, and he hadn't changed a bit since. "You owe me. And you can't imagine how much my buddies would like some payback, too. *If* they could find you."

"You were all convicted because you were dealing drugs, Allan. It wasn't because of me." She fought off a familiar wave of regret. Her life would've been so different if he hadn't come along. "You got what you deserved."

"My friends and I think different." His tone grew silky. "It wouldn't have cost you a nickel to say the right things to the cops."

"I was honest."

"Honest?" He swore softly. "Whatever. The guys and I weren't the only ones using, sugar."

"Because you made sure you dragged me right down with you…and I was naive and stupid enough to follow. But I paid the price."

"Three years' probation was *nothing* compared to incarceration."

"Look, I'm done talking to you about this. It's over. Don't call again, understand?"

"Done? I don't think so. Don't make me come after you again."

"Your threats were documented by the cops years ago. If there's any trouble here, they'll know who to go after." She took a steadying breath. "So don't even try."

"Then send me a thousand bucks, Krissie. I—I'm in a little trouble, here."

"I can't. I don't have it."

"Sure you do." His voice dropped to a flat whisper. "Especially since you'd like to find Emma, right?"

She inhaled sharply. "You know where she is? Is she all right?"

"I…have friends who've seen her."

She heard the slight hesitation in his voice, and knew he was hedging. Still…

"I don't believe you." Kris gripped the cell phone tighter, her fingers turning numb.

"I figured as much, so I asked them to give me some proof." He snickered. "She said she's real sorry about that swing-set incident when you were seven. She didn't mean to hurt you like that. Good enough?"

Kris touched the tiny, crescent-shaped scar at her temple. *I probably told him about the scar myself, years ago. Or did I?*

"Tell me where she is. Please."

"Maybe next time." He rattled off the name and phone number of a drugstore. "If you're real good. Send the money by wire, babe. I need it today. And I promise, I'll pay you back."

FOUR

Trace had been pleasant, if not exactly friendly, during his visit yesterday. He'd made it clear that his presence was a favor to his sister and nothing more.

Yet, to Kris's surprise, he appeared the following morning at seven and the morning after, with two ranch hands who helped him begin repairing the fence line surrounding the property. When she offered to help, he just gave her a dry smile and nodded toward the kennel. "Only you can decide what to do with all the stuff in there. We'll take care of this."

On Saturday they came once again, and by the time they headed for the ranch pickup, the split-rail fence was finished and the tumbledown corrals out by the barn were in good repair.

She caught up to him as he and his men were climbing into the truck. "I can't thank you enough," she said, a little breathless from the altitude and the deep snow.

"No problem," he said with a shrug, standing at the

open driver's-side door. "Couldn't have done it during the winter if the posts hadn't been good, but fixing the rails was easy."

"Well, believe me—what you did was beyond my skill set. Can I at least offer you guys lunch? Supper?"

The cowboys on the other side of the truck exchanged hopeful looks, but Trace shook his head. "We've got to put together a load of cattle this afternoon. But thanks anyway." He hiked a thumb toward his companions. "That's Rex Talbot on the left and Wiley Miller, by the way. They've been with me for five or six years. You might see one or the other now and again."

Rex, tall and lanky with a perpetual grin, dipped the brim of his hat. "The boss says we oughta check in on you if we're in the area, ma'am."

Surprised and touched by Trace's thoughtfulness, she tilted her head to study the faint color climbing up Trace's neck. "That's awfully nice of you."

"Just neighborly." He climbed behind the wheel, and without another word, the three men left.

Interesting. Trace had barely spoken to her during any of his visits, yet he'd donated a sizable amount of time to helping a stranger. Was this just a modern-day example of the old code of the West, or did he have a softer side that he didn't want to reveal?

"Hey, boss. You going all soft over that little lady next door?" Wiley nudged Rex on the ribs as the two of them piled out of the pickup back at the Rocking R. "I think that filly has caught his eye, don't you?"

"Being neighborly," Trace shot back. "And that's it."

"Not from where I was standin'. You seemed mighty interested whenever she showed up."

"Neighbors," Trace said firmly.

"She's sure a looker. Why, if I was free, I'd be chasing after her for sure."

"Me, too," Rex chimed in. "You wouldn't have a chance, boss. I'd take her out to the Twisted Spur every weekend, and dance up a storm."

Trace snorted. "I'm sure a classy woman would just love an offer like that. How you two ever managed to find those good women of yours escapes me."

Rex laughed and swept off his hat, revealing a shock of red hair. "Guess I'm tall, dark and handsome. How Wiley did it I'll *never* know."

Wiley snorted. "Pure charm. Just like them fellas on the TV. Anyone with two eyes could see that."

"Well, you two can go out and charm the two-year-old colts this afternoon," Trace drawled. "Start them off in the arena, then take them up in the hills and put some miles on them. I've got to work in the office this afternoon."

The ranch hands nodded and sauntered off to the barn, trading good-natured insults on the way. Trace turned on his heel and headed for the ranch office up at the house.

The boys were dead wrong. He'd been sending them over to work at Kris's place day after day because she was alone and she needed help…and because Thalia would have liked the fact that neighbors were pitching in to clean up her beloved home. It was what Thalia herself would've done for anyone else.

If he'd appeared to show any interest in Kris, it had been wholly unintentional.

It had nothing to do with her slender figure, or the way her eyes lit up when she talked about her hopes for the future.

Or her gentle, loving touch with her old dog, showing a side of her that she mostly kept hidden.

Some men liked their women soft and sweet like pretty clinging vines who wanted someone to shelter them and make every decision. But after growing up with a mother and sister like his, Trace found strength more appealing than just a pretty face, and dogged determination more appealing than any silvery laugh or flashing, flirtatious smile.

Kris had all of those qualities in spades.

But Wiley's and Rex's comments had doused the embers of interest that had started flickering in his midsection as neatly as if they'd dropped a bucket of ice water over his head.

He strode into the house, down the hallway to his office and settled behind his desk, where stacks of livestock records and invoices and bills awaited him.

They'd been joking. It didn't mean a thing, but it was still a reminder of the road he'd been down not long ago. His fiancée and a trusted friend had headed off into the sunset together without so much as a second glance back.

* * *

Seeing Wind Hill Ranch through the eyes of a county inspector made Kris realize she still had a long, long way to go.

Erwin Foster, a slender man with a tidy David Niven mustache and a shock of white hair, stalked through the kennel and barn with a clipboard in hand, writing pages upon pages of notes.

He'd told her to just sit tight until he finished, so she'd been pacing the confines of the small office in the kennel for the past hour, her arms wrapped around her middle to contain the butterflies trying to escape. Now, watching him heading her way with a grim expression on his face, she prepared herself for the worst.

"Well," he said, tapping his pen against the clipboard. "You requested a preliminary report, but I'm afraid you've got a long ways to go before we can even consider this place."

"I expected that. Do I have much competition?"

"With the local economy the way it is, the chance for a good income has a lot of people interested. One fella's place is nearly up to code already…and a couple others seem pretty desperate."

Disappointment washed through her, and it took a moment for her to find her voice. "Thanks so much for your time, then."

"Hold your horses. I didn't say you should give up."

"But—"

"You have a good, central location, which would save the county money on transportation costs. This property has a number of other advantages, including the barn, which would be helpful if the county needed to rescue any larger animals." He gave her a long, measuring look. "If you can make the most crucial improvements and schedule a full inspection in the next thirty days, you'll have a good chance at the contract. Two weeks would be even better."

She swallowed. "Two *weeks?*"

He pulled a carbon copy of his inspection form from his clipboard and handed it to her, along with a stapled set of state animal-shelter regulations. "A few of the problems involve outside work that can't be done until after spring thaw, but we could allow a temporary permit in the meantime. There's still quite a list—starting with fixing the furnace and the water heater, and issues with the plumbing and electrical wiring. Of course," he added, waving a hand toward the pens, "the dog runs need to be repaired and the broken windows replaced."

Her heart grew heavier with every noncompliance issue she read on the list. "I'm not sure I can afford to hire enough help to get it done in time. I don't even know who to call."

"Like I said, times have been tough around here this winter. There hasn't been much work, so I think you'll get some reasonable bids from guys who would do a good job." He chewed on the end of his pen for a moment, then jotted several names on a scrap of paper and handed it to her. "These names aren't an official recommendation, you understand. You can ask for more references at the hardware store."

"Understood."

All too well. With just a few thousand dollars in her savings, did she dare gamble it on the future, or should she play it safe? But when would she ever have another opportunity like this one?

Feeling a surge of hope, she extended her hand to shake his. "I appreciate your advice. I'm going to work 24/7, and do whatever I can, so maybe this place *will* be ready to pass your inspection, the next time around."

As soon as the inspector left, Kris started calling. The first two guys on the inspector's list were booked until spring. The third, a handyman named Herb from Battle Lake, was a retired contractor with a variety of skills. He was not only available thanks to a job cancellation but was well-versed on building codes and didn't seem daunted by the long list of corrections.

While Herb worked on the furnace, electrical problems and water heater, Kris cleaned and painted and took more trips to the landfill, then she helped him repair the dog runs.

She'd had only enough money to pay him for two weeks, though Carrie and her brother had come over several evenings to wield paintbrushes and hammers, and Polly—just out of the goodness of her heart—had shown up to lend a hand almost every evening after her store closed.

Now Kris stood shoulder to shoulder with Herb as they studied the interior of the kennel.

The walls were painted gloss white—easy to clean.

The two rooms at the end, one for cat cages and the other for pocket pets, were scrubbed and painted. A fund drive in town over the weekend, spearheaded by Carrie, had yielded a wide variety of cages for the smallest pets, as well as a good assortment of pet food for the supply room.

And—something Kris could only assume was an answer to her prayers and some well-placed calls from Polly or Carrie—a vet on the verge of retirement donated a dozen stainless-steel cat cages from his old clinic. Added to the animal rescue truck and the equipment the county had promised her, her facilities were all set to go.

"It all looks wonderful," Kris said. "I can't believe it."

"We don't have that last inspection report back, yet," Herb said dourly.

She glanced at her watch. "The inspector said he'd be here over an hour ago with his report. Do you think that means bad news or good?"

The door opened behind them and Erwin Foster stepped inside with Carrie at his heels. She was almost vibrating with excitement and fighting back a grin she could barely contain.

Foster gave her a dry look. "I hope you never try to play poker. Maybe you just want to go ahead and say it?"

She playfully elbowed him. "Erwin is an old friend from church. I ran into him at the courthouse this morning, and when he told me, I just had to come along. You got it—the final report. You passed!"

She scurried forward to give Kris a hug, then turned

to give Herb a hug, too. The old man blushed and stammered as she stepped back.

"This is absolutely terrific." Kris reached forward to shake Foster's hand. "I just heard from the county board yesterday, and they said they'd give me a six-month provisional contract if this final inspection was approved. It's like a dream come true."

"Hmmph. Remember you said that when you're cleaning up after all those dogs," Herb muttered, though the twinkle in his eyes gave him away.

Erwin handed her an envelope. "Don't forget the *provisional* part. There are those other issues to be addressed after spring thaw, and you'll also be subject to unannounced inspections for compliance with state and county regulations. If there are problems, they'll have to shut you down."

"I understand. You won't be disappointed, I promise you that." Kris nodded at a three-inch binder on the table. "I've gone through the Battle Creek policy manual from cover to cover, and I've made some adjustments as this place will be privately run. But I can assure you that I'll maintain Polly's standards and the county regulations in every way."

The piercing look he gave her wasn't completely reassuring. "Just don't forget it. There are still people around who'd take over the contract in a heartbeat, if you aren't able to make this work."

The constant activity and hard work had kept Kris exhausted and distracted for two weeks.

After everyone left, she rolled the tension out of her shoulders, jogged out to the highway to pick up her mail from the mailbox at the end of the lane, then walked back to the house and collapsed on the sofa with Bailey in her lap.

"So far, so good, but it isn't over yet, buddy," she murmured. "Just look at this mess!"

Though most of the items stored in the kennels had been rusted, broken or water damaged and had been hauled to the landfill, some of the usable household goods had gone to Goodwill. The remaining boxes and piles of odds and ends had come into the house and now filled the living room.

The pervading, musty scent was nearly overpowering…yet the mystery of what some of those boxes contained had held her entranced for weeks.

At least she was fairly sure that no mice had hitchhiked inside, as Bailey had shown little interest in the boxes.

But all mystery aside, the place suddenly seemed…empty. All the more because Carrie had left with a jaunty wave, calling out that she had to go to Bozeman for a few days and that Trace was going with her.

With a deep sigh, Kris flipped through the thin stack of mail at her side. Bills. More bills. A flyer from the drugstore. A single business envelope without a return address.

Intrigued, she slid a fingernail under the flap. A bill from Herb, maybe?

But it wasn't an invoice.

It was a small, neatly folded paper bearing a brief, unsigned note.

No one wants you here. Coming back here was a big mistake. If you don't leave, you're gonna be real sorry.

Her heart caught in her throat as memories of another note came crashing back. Vivid images of blood and death and of a child who'd been buried in a shallow grave.

The cops said Laura's killer had died of a self-inflicted gunshot wound, with a written confession note in his hand, in a remote cabin in the mountains above Battle Creek.

Kris's nightmares should've been over after the news of his death, yet they still came back to haunt her at the most unexpected times. Rocking her sense of security. Making her startle at shadows.

The murder had changed her life in so many ways.

She paced the floor, debating. She would report the note to the sheriff, certainly, and then maybe she'd contact her old childhood friends. Though life had sent them all in different directions, Megan and Erin had been Laura's cousins and had probably stayed in better contact with each other than Kris had. Just talking things over would help.

They'd been such good friends, once upon a time, during those endless, lazy days of summer down in

Lost Falls. Swimming in the lake. Begging ice cream from Erin's grandma at Millie's General Store. Riding horses and playing softball, stretching out under the trees to share stacks of favorite books.

Until Kris's home life had fallen apart, that is. Her idyllic summer vacations had vanished after she and her younger sister began shifting through a string of foster homes in various parts of the county.

Soon afterward, Laura had died at the hands of a killer, and that had changed all four friends forever. Stunned and hurting, they'd clung to each other at first, but then they'd gone off to different schools, and they'd drifted apart.

Kris turned to the kitchen table, where a box of her personal possessions still sat, waiting to be unpacked, and she foraged through it until she found her address book. She'd planned to contact her old friends once she got settled here, but that couldn't wait any longer.

Erin had moved back to Lost Falls recently, thirty miles south of Battle Creek over rough mountain roads. Megan was nearly that far to the west, in Copper Cliff, over roads that were even worse…but she was a deputy in neighboring Marshall County, and she would know what to do.

She was definitely the one to call first.

FIVE

Two days later, as she was looking through more boxes, a flash of motion outside the front windows of the cabin made Kris launch to her feet. Her heart slowly settled back into place when she saw a Marshall County Sheriff's Department cruiser pull to a stop in the lane.

Since reading the anonymous letter, every sound, every movement she caught at the corner of her eye, had put her nerves on edge.

Which was ridiculous, she kept reminding herself.

Deputy Carlson had come out that evening, and had taken the note with him so he could run it for possible fingerprints. He'd also promised to stop in whenever he was in the area. And Bailey barked at every car that came onto the property, which made him a terrific early-warning alarm. Even if apparently fast asleep, he awoke and rushed to the door, barking madly unless he recognized the truck from the Rocking R.

And just this morning, an installation crew from Secure Homes had come out to put in a security system. A low-end model to be sure, though it still stressed her budget, but enough to safeguard the windows and doors on the main floor of the cabin. And a bold metal sign warning potential intruders of a security system was now at the end of the lane by the highway.

Once the kennel was up and running—if that day did come—she'd find a way to install security there, as well.

Now she heard the scrabbling of Bailey's toenails as he lumbered to his feet and galloped from the kitchen to the front entryway where he whined and clawed at the door.

"It's a friend," she murmured, resting a hand at his neck as she went to the door and opened it wide. She blinked against the harsh winter sunshine glaring off the blinding expanse of snow.

Bailey bounded outside and ran around the patrol car, his tail wagging as he sniffed at the tires, then he put his paws up on the passenger's-side rear door to peer in.

Megan stepped out and gave Kris a slight sad smile. "Guess he can tell this was a K-9 unit—even without my partner."

Sure enough—Kris looked down and saw the K-9 emblem under the words *Deputy Sheriff,* which were emblazoned across the entire side of the vehicle. The rear windows were darkened. "Where is he?"

Even in childhood, Megan had been the tough one of the group—neither bloody knees, taunts nor even Laura's death had made her cry. At least, when anyone else could see. But although she was still at least twenty feet away, Kris saw a brief tremble shudder through her before she visibly stiffened.

"Drug dealers. Almost a month ago." She bit out the words, her voice raw and hollow. "Vet couldn't save him."

"I'm so sorry." Kris strode out to the car, meeting her halfway to give her a comforting hug, but stepped back when she was jabbed in the stomach by something that felt like armor. *"Oh."*

"Yeah. Bullet-proof vest, badge, radio mike, and my service belt. Not exactly cuddly." The corner of Megan's mouth twisted up in a wry smile. "But I appreciate the thought."

Kris grinned in return. "It's great seeing you again, Meg."

"What's it been…at least ten, twelve years? You haven't changed a bit!"

"You either—except maybe for the weapons."

"I had to bring a prisoner to the Latimer County Jail, so it wasn't far out of my way to swing by. Erin is back, too, you know—she bought her grandma's store down in Lost Falls. I expect she'll be coming up to see you one of these days."

"It seemed like a whole different world back when we were kids," Kris said with a wistful sigh. "Did you know that I used to pretend I was your cousin, too? It

seemed like you all had such perfect lives, until..."
She couldn't voice the words, but their eyes locked in
a brief, painful moment of complete empathy.

"Laura's death. It changed us all." The brisk, almost
impersonal words belied the shadow of old sorrows in
Megan's eyes. "When I got your message, I figured I
ought to come see you instead of just calling."

"I know it's crazy, but at the first sign of trouble, I
thought about her killer."

Megan's short, decisive nod left no room for
question. "But he's definitely dead. There was a
written confession. DNA matched. What still makes
me angry is that he took the spineless way out—blew
his brains out just as the SWAT team was closing in
on him. He deserved to face a jury and hear every last
impact statement from the families he destroyed."

"Would it have made a difference?"

"To him, probably not. But maybe it would have
helped give closure to Laura's parents. To all of us."
Megan lifted a shoulder. "Personally, I wish I could
have stared that man down until he shook in his boots.
I've found forgiveness is not an easy road to follow
sometimes."

Kris nodded. "For you and me both. And when I got
that threatening note, everything just rushed back."

"Do you still have it?"

"A copy. A deputy took the original to check for
prints, but he called this morning and said there wasn't
anything to lift. The guy must have used gloves."

"So he's not entirely stupid, then."

"Come on inside, and I'll show it to you." Kris led the way across the porch and opened the door for Bailey and her old friend. Then she went to the desk she'd set up in a spare bedroom and retrieved the note. "See? He—"

"Or she."

"Right. It sounds like a threat from someone who knows I lived in Montana once before. But why would anyone care? I know I got in some trouble in high school when I lived around here, but I met my juvenile probation requirements, and those records were expunged when I turned eighteen."

Megan looked up and held her gaze. "And then you married Allan."

Kris stiffened. "I met him in college over in Boise. The people around here wouldn't know about what happened there…would they?"

"Maybe. These days, anyone with a computer, an Internet connection and twenty or thirty bucks can search legal records from their own home." Megan reached out to give her hand a quick squeeze. "Allan and his friends were bad, bad news. Someone could figure you were, too, since you did have a drug charge—even if you were never a dealer. Guilt by association and all that."

Kris felt her heart crumple over all that could never be erased. "Allan was one of my biggest mistakes, but I have to take responsibility, too."

"You never had it easy, though, especially after that crazy mom of yours took off."

Kris managed a wry laugh. "And then Allan came along. Dangerous. Handsome. Exciting. Sort of like my own James Dean, and I even thought he loved me."

She shut her eyes briefly, remembering the brief marriage that had spiraled into disaster. She'd been so awed when he singled her out at a college freshman dance, then promised her the moon during a whirlwind courtship.

She'd impulsively married him on her nineteenth birthday, and he'd promptly led her down his dark path into alcohol, then drugs, though she'd never guessed that he and his friends were fencing stolen property and dealing crack until a trio of cops appeared at their door. Allan—honorable guy that he was—had tried to implicate her and dodge the charges himself, claiming he had no idea that she was up to no good.

A Christian counselor at a free clinic had later helped her turn her life around, and ever since then, she'd tried to lead a good, Godly life. But even now, she was paying for her mistakes.

"Allan got three years, and he's been free for eight or so. I only hear from him when he wants money. I usually refuse."

"Usually?"

"I helped him out once, long ago. But the last time he called, he'd somehow learned about my inheritance and claimed to know something about Emma."

"How recently?"

"Maybe three weeks or so. He keeps saying that I 'owe' him, because I refused to lie to the police, and in court. But that's ridiculous. He deserved the sentence he got."

"From what you've told me, he's a selfish jerk, Kris. He *uses* people. I'll bet he knows nothing at all about Emma."

"I know." Kris sighed heavily. "I'd already resolved to never listen to him again, but just hearing her name gave me such a surge of hope. I'm so afraid that I'll miss the one chance to find her."

"What about his friends?"

Kris thought for a moment. "They got five to seven years, I think. But who knows—people get released all the time on one technicality or another. I barely knew them, and it was all part of a chapter in my life that I wanted to forget."

"What were their names again?"

"Jay…Jay Miller, and Tom…somebody."

Megan pulled a pen and small tablet from her shirt pocket and wrote some notes. "They won't be too hard to track down. I'll see if they've been released, and then I'll let you know what I find out."

Kris fought the urge to give her old friend another hug. "Thanks, Meg."

"No problem." Meg smiled. "What are best old friends for? I was always sorry that we drifted apart in high school. We were such good friends as kids."

"Moving through the foster-care system made it pretty difficult. In my junior year I landed with three different families. And Emma…" A wave of regret made Kris's words catch in her throat.

"There's nothing you could've done to change what she did. You two didn't even live together, and she made her own choices."

"Bad ones, much like mine. Underage smoking. Friends who spelled trouble. And then came her shoplifting charge, and being caught with pot at a high school football game."

Emma had landed in juvie, too, though her charges had been more serious, and she'd ended up being sent to a facility in another part of the state. Kris hadn't seen her since before her hearing.

Kris lifted her gaze to Megan's. "I don't suppose there's any chance that you could help me find her."

"Those records are sealed. You know that."

"Even to you?"

"Even to me. She's what—twenty-seven now? She could've changed her name. Married. Moved across the country. If she wanted to find you, she could do it easily enough, since you took back your maiden name."

The truth of Megan's words settled like a hard, cold weight in Kris's stomach. "True."

"Have you tried hiring a private investigator…or tried some of those Internet investigation sites?"

"I hired P.I.s twice…until my money ran out. And I did try Internet searches a couple times, but I came up completely dry."

"Maybe—" Megan's expression softened "—maybe there's a chance that she's beyond finding."

Her words, so gently spoken, still felt like the slice of a stiletto into Kris's heart. "I *know* she's alive. If I can find her, maybe I can help her. Give her a place to stay…find her the help she needs. Hey, there's sure plenty of room here."

Megan scanned the property, her gaze falling on the kennels and barns. "On the phone you mentioned wanting to run an animal shelter."

Kris shook off her melancholy thoughts. "I sent in the check yesterday, so the county should be sending me a provisional license pretty soon. It'll be a way to generate income so I can continue to update the place."

Megan tilted her head, considering. "But you still plan to sell?"

"At first, I figured on a few months for sprucing things up and selling it in the spring. Now, I'm hoping to operate a shelter here for the next year."

"Good girl. The county needs a place like this, believe me." She looked at her watch. "I've got to get back on the road. Are you going to be okay out here all alone?"

Kris laughed at that. "Bailey lets me know if *anything* comes on the property. I have neighbors, too—a gal and her brother who've been over quite a bit to help me out. And now, since I got that note, a deputy comes up the lane every now and then just to take a look. Between all of them, the guy I hired to help me with repairs and the new security system in the house, I should be all set."

Megan frowned. "Still…be careful. You're awfully

isolated here. In our county, we've had an upswing in meth labs and drug transport through the area. With hundreds of thousands of acres to cover and few deputies, it's hard to catch everything going on, and I know it's the same over here. I just wish you were in my jurisdiction, but you're not even close."

"You should go over and say hello," Carrie said. "You haven't been back for a whole *week*."

"I've sent my men over for a few hours every day, though."

"But *you're* her neighbor. You should stop in, too."

Carrie's intent, stern look was undoubtedly part of her teacher's arsenal, and if it was half as effective on young teens as it was on him, she was probably given considerable respect by the kids at Battle Creek Middle School.

He turned to the gelding he'd cross-tied in the aisle of the barn and settled a saddle blanket on its broad back. "I will…one of these days."

"Today, Trace. You've got time. That gelding could use the miles, in fact."

He made a noncommittal sound as he swung his saddle up and gently positioned it over the blanket.

"I'm not asking you to take her on a date. I'm just asking you to be *neighborly*."

Hadn't he been? He'd done what he could to help Kris clean up Thalia's place. He'd made sure she met Polly. Anything more might be misconstrued as personal interest, and he sure wasn't going *there*.

There were a dozen reasons why he should keep his distance…and all of them were far, far more important than the fact that Kris was one of the most attractive and intriguing women he'd ever met.

He reached under the horse to snag the cinch. When he straightened, Carrie was at his side. Her concern for him was palpable…and that was another area he didn't want to deal with. "I'll get over there…later today. Maybe tomorrow. Promise."

Carrie rested her hand on his arm. "You can't let that accident change your life. Do you think Bill—"

"Drop it, Carrie."

Being Carrie, she ignored him and shook her head. "It's been a *year*. He was one of your best friends, and he would've wanted you to move on."

The past weighed on his chest like a horseshoer's anvil—a cold, smothering weight that made it hard for his heart to beat.

Without sparing her a glance, Trace finished saddling the colt, slipped a snaffle bit into its mouth, gently looped the headstall over its head, then led the colt into the harsh sunshine glaring off the mounds of fresh snow.

Ignoring the old, aching pain in his left knee, he swung into the saddle and shook some slack into the reins, then headed out toward the five hundred acres of government land leased to the Rocking R.

Carrie was wrong.

During those last few moments in that rodeo arena—moments that had seemed like an eternity as

Trace watched the disaster unfolding—he'd prayed like never before.

But he hadn't made it in time.

Trace didn't deserve Bill's forgiveness...and his friend certainly hadn't had the chance to grant it at any rate. Maybe he was riding the ranges of heaven in peaceful bliss, but he sure hadn't deserved his violent death.

He should've been here on earth until his hair turned gray, tending his own ranch. His wife. His two kids.

And he would've been, if Trace hadn't let him down.

SIX

The colt—a big, black three-year-old Trace had nicknamed Rowdy—lived up to his name for the first half hour. On the long, plowed lane out to the highway he danced sideways, his neck arched and chin tucked, mouthing the snaffle bit and shaking his head.

He shied wildly at the rustle of an owl's wings in a tree high overhead. Startled at a downed log that had no resemblance whatsoever to a four-footed predator. Snorted and spun into a lightning fast rollback toward home when a fearsome rabbit appeared a good twenty feet away.

When they reached the highway, Trace made him stand quiet and still and, with a reassuring hand on the colt's neck, waited for a few cars to pass by.

At the first, Rowdy snorted and shied explosively, trying to spin and bolt for home. At the second and third, he blew noisily through his nostrils and pawed, then tried to back up. Each time Trace gently but persistently made him stay in place. It took another fifteen minutes for a fourth car to appear, but this time, Rowdy just watched, his muscles rock-hard with tension.

"So you're not gonna try to make a break for it this time? Good boy." Trace laid a rein lightly against the colt's neck, turning him toward a network of trails leading through the government land that lay between the Rocking R and Wind Hill Ranch to the south.

Good, rugged land for working the kinks out of a bow-backed colt with little experience and too much energy…which was the only reason Trace had chosen to go that way. That they were still heading south long after the colt quieted and got down to business had nothing to do with the new neighbor, either.

At least not much.

Though when the snow got deeper and the hills grew steeper, Trace finally debated about turning for home. What was he thinking? Saddling a green colt on a cold, windy day could be akin to cinching a keg of dynamite, but turning up too often at Wind Hill had the potential for more trouble than that.

He'd been all wrong, the first day they'd met. He'd thought Kris was "halfway attractive," but each time he saw her he seemed to see something new.

The way she set her chin when she was determined to get a job done and then just wouldn't quit, even when she looked exhausted.

The sparkle in those big green eyes…though they seemed to hold old ghosts, too, which made him wonder anew why a gal like her was here all alone and not settled down somewhere with a passel of kids and a white picket fence. Then again, maybe she already had someone patiently waiting for her, while she was taking care of her inheritance.

Which made perfect sense, come to think of it— all the more reason that getting too close to her wasn't a good idea. Not at all.

Yet…he still found himself riding on, as the trail wound down through a deep ravine, then back up through the thick pines to a boulder-strewn rise overlooking Thalia's place. The little pine-rimmed meadow was as pretty as a postcard, with that old log barn and cabin, and a backdrop of soaring mountain peaks. And though he'd half wished her SUV would be gone and he could just turn for home, it was there…and he could see her old dog out by the kennel.

Up here, he'd seen some footprints in the fresh snow, so she'd probably found some time to go exploring this morning. If she'd gotten this far, and had seen this view, how could she not want to stay in Montana forever?

"Since she's home, I guess we oughta say howdy," he murmured, stroking Rowdy's neck as he urged the colt forward.

"Just to make Carrie happy."

At the bottom of the hill he positioned Rowdy next to the gate so he could open it and get into the meadow. Still green, the colt danced in place, balked, then crowhopped when Trace leaned down again to shut the gate.

The old retriever had taken up a position on the cabin porch but now he came barreling across the meadow, barking furiously in full watch-dog mode.

Kris appeared at the door of the kennel. "Bailey! No!"

The dog kept coming, bounding through the deep snow.

Rowdy snorted, reared, scrambled to keep his footing on the icy slope, then crashed sideways into the fence, slamming Trace's left leg against a post. Blinding pain rocketed through Trace's bad knee and the world spun in an explosion of stars, then went dark.

"Trace? Trace!" Kris's voice came from far away.

He swallowed back a wave of nausea.

Blinked.

And found himself looking up into her worried face. A soft hand cradled the side of his jaw.

Startled, he blinked again and shook his head—and instantly regretted it. "I feel like I got hit with a sledge-hammer," he muttered when the throbbing pain faded. Alarm shot through him. "Where's my horse?"

"He seems fine." She held up a hand holding Rowdy's reins. "But I'm not so sure about you. He squashed your left leg against the fence. Then he slipped and went over backward, and slammed you against that tree next to the gate. It's a wonder you're not dead." She held up a cell phone. "I was just going to call 911."

"Don't." The snow beneath him was wet and cold,

but even so, he felt warmth creep up the back of his neck. "I'm fine."

"Right. After putting a dent in that poor tree with your head."

He knew she was kidding, but it hurt too much to smile.

On any other day he would have bailed in time. He would've been in control of the situation. But he'd been caught unaware when Rowdy crashed into the post—probably undoing two years of healing and more physical therapy appointments than he could count.

"I—I'll just get on my horse and be on my way. Got chores to do."

"Nuh-uh."

She leaned down to peer into his eyes and he caught the scent of her perfume...or maybe it was her shampoo. Light and lemony, reminding him of a spring day...

"Pupils are equal. No blood I can see. But people *die* from blows to the head, and I'm not having that on my conscience. Can you stand up?"

If it involved using his bad leg, maybe not...but he didn't want to admit to weakness around her, either. Gritting his teeth, he levered himself out of the snow, then crouched for a second.

She hooked an arm under his and helped him slowly rise to his feet. "Take it easy, cowboy."

She looked a little fuzzy, but maybe it was snowing. Was it snowing? "See? Fine. I'm just fine."

"I'm calling Carrie."

Alarm shot through him, and just like that, his brain cleared. If Carrie got wind of this, she'd be fluttering around him 24/7—just as she had after he'd come home from the hospital following the Denver rodeo, surgery and a month of rehab.

"Look, I'll just catch my breath for a few minutes, but nothing more than that—and *don't* call Carrie."

Kris wavered, then her eyes narrowed. "In that case, I'll take you to the house and keep an eye on you for a while. I've got empty box stalls in the barn, and thanks to you and Carrie, there's even some hay in there. I can give your horse a few leaves of alfalfa to keep him happy."

He forced himself to match her pace without limping, even though the pain in his knee escalated with every stride. By the time they reached the porch, he was sweating like he'd done a marathon in mid-summer.

"Does Rowdy ground tie?" Her gaze flicked between the horse and her front door.

"Nope."

"Can I tie him long enough to get you in the house?"

"Probably. Know how to tie a quick-release knot?"

She rolled her eyes. "Was I born in Montana?"

He considered, realizing that there was a *lot* he didn't know about her, and it now seemed like pretty fascinating stuff. "Guess I'm not sure."

"Well, I was, and I know how to tie a horse." She

swiftly tied a slipknot that could be released with a single tug of the free end, then ushered him into the kitchen and settled him in a chair. "Don't even think about moving. I'll be back in a flash."

The kitchen was warm, the pale yellow walls lit by winter sun streaming through the windows facing the back of the property. The rich scent of coffee filled the air, and he looked longingly at the coffeepot sitting on the counter.

She followed his gaze. "Nope. Not just yet."

She was as bossy as Carrie and his former fiancée combined.

Trace waited until she disappeared out the door, then used both hands to position his leg at a more tolerable angle. It was already starting to stiffen up, and as much as he hated to admit it, ending up in Kris's kitchen seemed like a good alternative to being on Rowdy's back right now.

Minutes later footsteps clomped up the back porch, and she walked in with her dog at her heels, watching Trace intently as she peeled off her heavy down jacket and kicked off her snowboots, then released her long, sunstreaked hair from her navy stocking cap. Her cheeks were rosy from the cold.

Bailey circled a few times and then curled up in front of the refrigerator. Kris poured a half cup of coffee and stood across the table from him, cradling it in her hands instead of handing it over. "You're feeling okay?" When he nodded, she added, "You're *sure?*"

He cracked a smile, and dredged up his best country charm. "I'll be good when I thaw out…and that coffee would sure help, ma'am."

She handed it over. "This whole thing is against my better judgment."

"I got bucked off of worse bulls and broncs in my day. One green colt is nothing."

"You *rodeo?*"

Her voice held none of the awe he'd inspired in the cute little buckle bunnies who'd frequented the rodeo circuit. He gave her a wary look over the rim of his coffee cup. The last thing he wanted to do was talk about his rodeo career—or the end of it. "Uh…yeah. I did."

Resting a hip against the counter, she folded her arms. "Travel a lot?"

"Not anymore."

"I'll bet that was a hard transition."

He shrugged. "I cashed in my savings, bought a ranch, and came back to Montana."

"You didn't grow up on the Rocking R?"

"My dad had a ranch not too far from here. But his health failed early and with one thing or another, he had to sell out when I was barely in high school."

"So you turned to rodeo."

Trace gave a self-deprecating laugh. "To a kid living on a failing ranch, rodeo was filled with glamour and excitement. The adventure of the open road, prize money and all that."

"You must've done well, to buy a ranch."

He shrugged. "The first few years were hand-to-mouth—sharing a truck and gas money with two other guys. Sleeping in back-lot stalls, living on fast food and dreams."

"Some of my friends dated rodeo cowboys, but they were bad news, with big dreams, then bad excuses for all the times they didn't come back home when expected, or were out carousing. When one was photographed for a rodeo magazine with his arm around some little cowgirl, it nearly broke my friend's heart. He was just like all of his wild pals."

The guy had been blind, if the girl had been anything like Kris. "Well, I wasn't like that. And none of my buddies were, either."

She didn't look convinced, and it shouldn't matter what she thought. He was hardly here trying to wrangle himself a date. Yet at the doubt in her eyes, he found himself wanting to prove her wrong. "A lot of guys I know belong to a Christian rodeo cowboy association. Most of them are dead serious about success in the year-end standings, and for that you need the focus of an athlete."

She nodded. "It's a hard life, I know."

If only she knew. "A body can take just so much before it starts catching up to you. So now I raise bucking stock, quarter horses and cattle." He drained the last of his coffee, then glanced at his watch. "And speaking of that, I need to get on my way."

"Let me give you a ride home. You could get your horse later."

From outside came the sound of tires crunching through the snow. Glancing out the window, he could see a van stop by the kennel. A trio of little girls poured out of the side door the second it opened.

"Looks like you've got business, anyway. How are things going?"

She laughed. "Like a landslide. In the first forty-eight hours I had two litters of kittens and four stray dogs brought in. Since then, two cats and another dog, plus a guinea pig named Mittens who whistles at everyone who walks by. There've been three adoption forms filled out so far." She hesitated. "The bad part is that I've gotten a couple of anonymous calls about someone running a puppy mill, but the caller didn't give the guy's name—just the name of a gravel road that crosses the entire county."

At the image of her facing down some irate man, he felt a distinct rush of unease. "The caller should've contacted the sheriff, not you. Don't go checking on that place by yourself."

A faint tinge of pink darkened her cheeks. "I actually did go out looking, a couple times. I drove slowly, and covered maybe twenty miles of that road looking for anything suspicious. I'd like to give the sheriff's office something more concrete than information from an anonymous caller."

Trace winced at the thought of her out there, all alone. "Some of those places are terrible, and the owners could be mighty defensive about someone snooping around."

She rolled her eyes. "I *wasn't* snooping, and I'm not careless. I reread the old procedure manual, then called the sheriff's office. Apparently one of the deputies is supposed to go check it out, but I haven't heard anything."

"Did you check your caller ID?"

"For the person with the complaint? The screen just read Unavailable."

Trace rose and shouldered on the coat he'd hung on a peg at the back door. "If they send Ken, I'm sure he'll take care of it. I don't know the other two deputies very well. They're fairly new."

Kris pulled on her coat, too. "Be careful going home, okay?"

"Yes, ma'am." He pulled on his gloves. "Pretty view of your place from the crest of that first hill, isn't it?"

"I'll have to check it out someday."

"You haven't? On my way here, I thought I saw your footprints up there."

She paled. "Footprints? I've never been hiking up that way. Not even once."

At the alarm in her eyes, he offered an offhand grin. "Probably just hikers. We've got some real hard-core people in these parts. Off-season campers, snow-shoers, you name it."

Her gaze skittered toward the dense timber framing the meadow. "This far out?"

"It's possible. I'll take another look on my way home. With this latest snow, it'll be real easy to see

where they came from and where they went." He hesitated. "If you ever get edgy about being here alone,
call me. Or you can just come on over—Carrie has an
extra bedroom in her cabin, and she loves company."

The brief cloud of worry in Kris's eyes vanished
and she offered him a blazing smile. "No need. But
thanks for the offer. I'll be absolutely fine."

Maybe she thought so, but he'd lived in these parts
too long to take safety for granted. And if those tracks
up on the hill revealed anything suspicious, he'd be
calling the sheriff, then heading back to watch over her
until further help arrived.

SEVEN

While Kris welcomed her visitors, Trace limped over to the barn, got back on his horse and rode off, stubborn man.

She thought back and realized that he'd favored that leg from the first time they'd met, though he clearly tried to hide it. Maybe he just didn't like sympathy and attention, but now it was too obvious to mask. Could he stand the discomfort of the long ride home? What if Rowdy spooked again?

Kris kept an eye on him as he rode out of sight, then turned again to the young couple waiting for her outside the kennel entrance. Their children—all grade-school age—eagerly watched her approach.

"We need a kitty!" the youngest girl burst out, hopping from one foot to the other. "Our Poppet ran away and made us all really sad. We need a white one!"

Her middle sister vehemently shook her head. "Orange. My favorite color is orange."

"An' I want a fluffy one, like a teddy bear." The oldest girl's expression was somber. "Like Poppet."

Their mother shushed them all. "Sorry. We've waited a couple months, but my husband and I think it's time. Do you have any kittens available?"

Kris surveyed all of the eager young faces and smiled. "I think I might be able to help. You do know there's a waiting period?"

The father nodded. "Same as at the old place—three days?"

"The previous board had increased it to four, I'm afraid. They were concerned about snap decisions and regrets that could leave an animal at risk. And I had to promise the county that I would follow the protocols set by the Battle Lake facility."

He hesitated at the door. "What do you think, June? Maybe we should look in the want ads. There always seem to be free kittens there."

"Maybe there'll be more in the spring, but I haven't seen any lately." The young woman swatted her puffy mittens together. "Brrr—let's go inside."

Kris ushered them into the building, then led them to the room reserved for cats and opened the door. "We have two litters here, actually. They were brought in just this week, and they're old enough to adopt."

The little girls squealed with delight as they hurried to kneel in front of a pen where an assortment of kittens were tumbling with each other, napping or climbing the wire.

Above their excited chatter, their father caught

Kris's eye. "What about health papers, and such? And the price?"

Kris lifted a clipboard from a hook on the wall, pulled off the top sheet, and handed it to him. "These little guys are all eight weeks. A vet is stopping by on Friday to give them exams and fecal tests for worms, and then they'll have their first shots and be spayed or neutered two weeks after that."

"But they're so *little,*" June exclaimed.

"I thought that too, at first, but it's very common these days—especially with shelter animals. Studies show no difference in growth, behavior or urethral problems. And it's unbelievable how fast cats can multiply—or how young." She nodded at the paper. "The statistics and research articles are cited on the back, along with the contract that would need to be signed."

"Contract?" the husband snapped.

"Stating that you'll promise to neuter your new pet."

"So we'd have to bring the kitten back here?"

"Yes, or I'd give you a coupon covering the entire cost if you want to use your own vet. The cost is factored into the adoption fees."

"And we'd also have that four-day wait. You can't make an exception? Look at our girls—they're so excited."

The sharp note in his voice set her on edge, but she dredged up a warm, apologetic smile. "If I bent the rules once, I'd have to do it for other people, and I could lose my county contract. Let's see, girls—does anyone want to hold a kitten? Be gentle, though…nice and quiet."

Over the din of excited voices Kris brought out the top choices and settled them gently into the girls' arms. "There's one you all missed, though. Look in the basket." She reached in and pulled out a sleepy, long-haired calico. She held it aloft, then handed it to their mother. "What do you think?"

"It gots white," the littlest girl said reverently.

The middle child grinned. "And orange!"

"And long fur like Poppet," the oldest girl murmured, her eyes filling with tears. "Please, Momma, can it be that one?"

"She *is* perfect, isn't she?" June nuzzled the kitten's downy coat. "What do you think, Ray?"

Her husband took a step back. "I think it's time for us to leave. Let's go, girls. We'll talk about it in the car."

"But Daddy!"

"Please!"

The chorus of little voices grew louder.

"Really now, Ray—where will we find one this perfect? I think—"

"I think we'll be on our way."

Stunned, Kris gathered up all the kittens and put them back in the cages, then watched the man herd his wailing children down the aisle. His wife looked back, her expression filled with regret and apology.

Ray waited until they were all through the door, then turned back. "I appreciate your time, miss."

"Is something wrong?"

His mouth flattened. "There were other applicants in the county for the shelter, you know. And some weren't very happy that it went to you. Not happy at *all*. Now I see why."

Taken aback at his vehemence, Kris stared at him. "I don't understand."

"Delays. High fees. Fancy rules." Ray snorted. "This is a little rural shelter, not some highfalutin place in New York City. I'm sure you won't be in business for long."

"The rules were in place at the previous facility, and I have to follow them here. Anyone operating a shelter in this county would."

"This place isn't *owned* by the county. You could sure make an exception if you wanted to. People aren't gonna be pleased over how you run this place, if you can't serve the public's needs." He walked out the door and let it slam shut behind him. A moment later, the minivan started with a roar of its engine.

She listened to it pull away, then held up the calico kitten cradled in her hands and looked into its face. Marked with a rakish dark patch over half its face, it looked for all the world like a fluffy pirate.

"That was a close call, little one," she murmured. "Those little girls were sweet, but I don't think you'd want to deal with their dad again."

But she might—and the county board of supervisors, as well, if he lodged a complaint. She'd only done her job, and she'd managed to remain calm and professional. But there were no witnesses, and what the guy would tell them about her was anyone's guess.

A rusty prayer found its way to her lips, and she closed her eyes. *Please, God, help me out here—please don't let him sabotage this place before I've even begun.*

Rowdy snorted and tossed his head when Trace stopped him at the top of the hill to study the tracks in the snow. The colt's impatience escalating now that he was headed for home, he started dancing in place, muddying the tracks.

But the direction was clear enough.

One set of tracks coming from the direction of the highway. One set of tracks going back. Big tracks— larger than Kris's small feet. Tracks that ended at the top of the hill looking over her place, though how long the guy had lingered and why he'd been there was unclear.

Photographers could be found out in the woods every season of the year. Campers. Hikers. Bird-watchers. The reason that someone had been up here could be as innocuous as a hiker losing the trail…but the feeling in Trace's gut told him otherwise.

The line of tracks was straight as an arrow to the top of this hill. Made with clear purpose, not a mean-dering search.

Wincing, Trace dismounted and draped one rein over the colt's neck, then held the other as he hunkered down to sift through the snow for anything the tres-passer might have left behind. *Nothing.*

He straightened, his knee creaking in protest. Rowdy nickered, tossing his head as he sidestepped to look toward home, but Trace kept circling the small area, kicking at clumps of snow with the toe of his boot. Surely there'd be something….

Finally, resigned, he turned back to the colt and put his foot in the stirrup. Something glittered beneath a ray of sunshine filtering through the dense pine branches above.

Trace stepped back down and reached for it. It was a crumpled cigarette package, shiny and new. He bent down and ran his hands through the snow.

Five cigarette butts.

Six.

An empty matchbook.

Given the depth of the snow, there could be even more cigarette butts here…but what he'd found indicated that someone had come up here and had stayed for a long while. Watching Wind Hill Ranch from a good vantage point? Why?

Still, the footprints could've been from a hiker.

Or someone hoping to photograph wolves or elk. On the darker side, maybe someone was trying to poach out of season.

As soon as he got home, he would mention it to the sheriff, to see if poachers had been active in the area…or if any DNR people were doing some conservation department research out here.

The footprints probably meant nothing…nothing at all. But he'd failed a close friend once before, and the searing pain of that unforgiveable failure had branded his heart forever.

And there was no way he was going to let anything slip past him again.

Kris moved through the kennel the next morning, feeding the animals and cleaning pens. Outside the sun had risen in a blaze of oranges and pinks over the foothills to the east, and with the promise of highs in the fifties, she could already hear the steady drip of snow melting from the roof.

"Mid-March, and you just never know," she said, stopping to stroke Bailey's head as she worked her way down the long aisle. "A blizzard or balmy. Take your pick."

"I'll take balmy."

Surprised, she turned at the familiar voice and found Trace sauntering down the aisle toward her, his hat at his side. "Did you ride over here again?"

"Drove. Do you have a minute?"

"Of course."

He stopped in front of her, smelling of snow and pine and leather, his thick black hair tousled. He looked like the epitome of tall, dark and masculine, but his mouth was again set in a grim line, and she found herself wondering what he'd look like if he ever broke into laughter. Probably drop-dead gorgeous and well out of her league, though she'd likely never find out. There was clearly something about her that he disliked, maybe even resented. And if not for Carrie's prodding, he certainly wouldn't have returned to Wind Hill a second time.

"I took a look at those tracks on my way home yesterday."

Despite his attitude, she continued to find the man way too attractive, but now those thoughts fled as a sense of unease made her shiver. "And?"

"They started down at the highway and ended up on that hill overlooking this place. Big prints, most likely a man's. He must've been up there for quite a while—he smoked a lot of cigarettes before heading back down to the highway." Trace studied her intently. "Have you had any unusual calls, or visitors lately? Any evidence of prowlers?"

"N-no…just people coming and going because of the shelter. No one who seemed suspicious." She bit her lip, thinking. "Bailey would pick up on any strangers around the house at night, and he'd bark his head off. And if anyone came around the kennel after dark, the shelter dogs would go crazy, too."

"I called the sheriff yesterday evening. He doesn't know of any DNR studies going on out here, and there haven't been any problems with poachers in the area. It's probable that the tracks were from someone out hiking or taking photos of wildlife."

But Trace didn't *look* as if he thought it was nothing. He looked flat worried about something, and it wasn't just some hiker or a townie with a camera. "With government lands close by and the tourism in this area, it wouldn't surprise me a bit."

"I told the sheriff he needs to be running a deputy through this area more often, but he's short staffed with one guy off on sick leave. Most ranchers around here carry at least one rifle on a rack in their pickups. Do you have one?"

"Th-there's a Winchester 700 .270 in the kennel office. It was Thalia's—it even has her initials carved on the stock."

"Do you know how to use it?"

She managed a slight smile. "I grew up in Montana, remember? I'm pretty rusty, but long ago I did stay with people who taught me."

"Do you carry your cell phone with you all the time?"

His intent gaze lasered into her own, making her shiver in an entirely different way. Flustered, she ducked her head and patted her pockets until she found her cell and took it out to show him. "Got it."

"Don't take any chances, hear?"

"I really don't think—"

"You know there was a break-in out here after Thalia died. We scared those guys off, but maybe they cased the house and will try to come back."

Or the prowlers could be from her own past.

Allan, maybe…or his friends. Or the person who'd left a threatening note in the mailbox. Maybe even someone from around here, who was in financial straits and resentful because she'd managed to snag the shelter contract and salary, though none of those ideas seemed likely.

A stronger possibility made her shiver.

The thought of dogs suffering at the hands of some greedy puppy mill breeder had made it impossible to sit still after she closed the animal shelter office yesterday, and there'd still been no word from the sheriff about him taking time to investigate.

So once again, she'd gone out to cover another long section of that road—cruising slowly enough to survey every property she passed, mile after mile. Anyone passing her surely would've mistaken her for a gawking tourist, but there hadn't been anyone else out there.

At least, no one she'd seen.

Dense underbrush had crowded one narrow lane marked with a dented mailbox. And there, she'd heard the faint sound of distant barking. A cacophony of barking…far more than the usual two or three dogs found on a ranch.

She hadn't been stupid. She'd taken note of the location, then kept going until she hit an area with good cell-phone reception, and she'd reported the place to the sheriff's office. He hadn't called back.

She pulled her thoughts back to the present when she realized Trace was giving her a curious look, and tried to remember what he'd just said. "I…appreciate your concern."

"I can be here in no time, if I'm at the ranch. Day or night. Unless," he added with a rueful smile, "I'm in the middle of a difficult foaling like I was last night."

"Did everything go all right?"

The corner of his mouth kicked up a notch. "Healthy colt, and the mare's fine, though she was a maiden mare and didn't want to accept him at first after all she went through during delivery."

Kris pulled a face. "Poor little guy."

"Stop by and see him sometime. We've got four new ones now. Three of them fillies, fortunately— and good paint color on all of 'em."

It wasn't a warm extension of friendship, exactly, but given the rocky start they'd had and his persistent, distant attitude, it was a step forward. *Polite neighbors…that's all I want to be, and nothing more.*

"I'd like that. Thanks." The cell phone in her hand chirped, and she automatically glanced at the unfamiliar number on the screen. She muted the ring and shoved the phone into her pocket. "Sorry—I'll return the call later."

Trace shook his head and turned toward the door. "Go ahead and take it. I need to get going, anyway. Just remember what I said…and watch your back."

EIGHT

The message on her voice mail was from a Deputy Sam Martin. His words sent adrenaline rushing through her, making her fingers tremble as she returned his call.

Thirty minutes later, Kris was behind the wheel of the Battle Creek shelter's old four-wheel-drive truck, bouncing over a series of rutted back roads that led far into the woods east of town.

Ahead, she could make out a county patrol car partially hidden by the heavy pine branches spilling over into the road. As she stopped by a familiar rusted mailbox, the lanky, redheaded deputy climbed out and waved her over to the side.

She rolled down her window as he approached her truck. "This is the place?"

"Yep. You were right about the puppy mill tip. The Bascombs are gone, far as I can tell. But they've been served a warrant. They knew we'd be coming."

Uneasiness crawled up her spine as she looked

down the narrow, gloomy lane. There were tire tracks through the snow, but thick brush crowded both sides and even in broad daylight it seemed dark and menacing. "Someone actually lives back there?"

"Harvey Bascomb and his son." Sam surveyed the area, his stance wary. "He's actually a second cousin of mine, and I know he isn't gonna like this—not at all. But I've got my orders, and I'd guess there'll be lawyers hashing it all out later. Come on."

He turned on his heel, climbed back in the cruiser, and drove slowly ahead of her down the lane.

Stiff branches clawed at the side of the truck, and deep ruts hidden by the snow grabbed at the tires. A half mile in the lane opened into a small clearing with a house and several long kennel buildings that had seen better days. A dilapidated old Chevy Mustang was parked by the house, its tires gone and hood raised. Snow filled the engine cavity.

The deputy pulled to a stop by the closest kennel and waved her over to the door. From inside the building rose a cacophony of frantic barking.

She stepped outside and rubbed her upper arms, feeling a sudden chill despite her jacket.

"Well," the deputy growled. "Let's get to it."

He led the way into the building, felt along the wall and flipped several switches. A single bare bulb flared to life in the center of a long aisle. The stench of filthy cages and—perhaps infected flesh—assaulted Kris's nose, and she retched.

Dozens of dogs, some of them two and three to a

narrow run, barked and jumped at the wire mesh doors of the pens. But though she'd expected them to be fierce, most seemed desperate, as if struggling to escape. From what she could see, at least half a dozen had been nursing pups recently.

"But there aren't any puppies! Where could they be?"

"Got me. Maybe he sold 'em." The deputy shoved a handful of leashes into her hand, his expression filled with doubt. "Let's get moving on this."

She swallowed and nodded, hoping she looked more confident than she felt. If Bascomb's own blood relatives were leery of him, what kind of man *was* he?

"This place was once known for champion field-trial dogs," Sam added. "So these animals were probably handled quite a bit. We should be okay. But let's get out of here fast as we can."

She gingerly moved down the aisle until she found a pen holding two emaciated dogs that were less crazed than the rest. "Let's start with you two," she murmured softly. She waited until they warily approached the front of their pen and let them cautiously sniff at her hand. "See? I'm a good guy. Let's get you out of here."

Unlocking the gate, she reached in and snapped leashes onto their collars. Whining, they both pulled back, their eyes rimmed with white. She sweet-talked them until they tentatively edged forward. At the front of their cage they jerked back again, as if terrified to leave, then finally followed her, their heads low and tails between their legs.

It was only when she got them out to the truck that she realized part of the stench had followed them outside.

Both dogs were crusted with filth, both had weeping sores over their jutting hipbones. She fought back a wave of nausea. *Oh, dear Lord...how can this be?* And what about the puppies—had they been just as bad?

But surely not. If Bascomb had raced off with them, hurrying to sell them, he'd hardly have much success unloading them at reputable pet stores if the puppies looked ill. Her stomach pitched. Unless they were headed for far worse circumstances.

The deputy followed with two other mature dogs, and they worked together to gently lift the animals into the individual cages built into both sides of the truck.

"This is just...just unbelievable," she murmured, listening to the four dogs scrambling to escape their new enclosures. "I saw some terrible things when I worked for another shelter, but nothing like this."

Sam's face was ruddy with exertion. "The Bascombs are good people. They just hit hard times."

"Good people?" Aghast, she stared at him. Even if they were his relatives, how could he excuse their deplorable care of these animals?

"There's more to the story than what you see, but we've gotta follow orders."

It took over an hour to search all of the outbuildings and rescue the remaining dogs. By the time the last one was safely secured, the odor of filthy kennels and festering sores hung like a miasma around the truck.

Over at his patrol car, the deputy tapped the microphone clipped to his shoulder, spoke into it, then he reached into the vehicle and withdrew an envelope.

"Here you go," he called out. "This is a copy of the court documents on this seizure, in case you need proof."

She accepted the envelope. "A thirty-day hold before they can be adopted, right?"

He nodded. "Board and vet costs paid by the county. The owners can go to court and contest the order…or clean up their facilities and reapply for a kennel license. Everything is down in black and white."

"Some of those animals are going to need significant veterinary care, from what I see."

"I think there's a ceiling cost per dog, unless you apply in writing for additional funds. In other words, no major surgery bills without approval."

"And in an emergency?"

"Call the vet. The sheriff tells me she worked with the old shelter. She knows the ropes."

The deputy shot an uneasy glance toward the driveway, and Kris took a closer look at him. Beneath his veneer of authority he was much younger than she'd first thought…and if he was uncomfortable about a potential encounter with the Bascombs, then she wanted to be on her way, as well.

She nodded her thanks and returned to the truck.

"I expect Harvey will come by to check on his dogs, but you shouldn't have any trouble," Sam called out to her. "Like I said, he was given notification about the complaints, and was also served with the court order. He's too smart to risk any more legal difficulties."

Kris climbed behind the wheel of the truck and locked the doors, then surveyed the property as she turned on the ignition. Did people really live in that spooky, dilapidated old house? And how could they allow such neglect of any animals—much less field-trial dogs that were probably worth a mint?

Shivering, she shifted the truck into gear and followed the deputy. She sighed with relief when the patrol car stopped at the highway, then turned left. *Home free.*

She turned on her right blinker, waiting for several cars and a pickup to pass. The cars whizzed by.

The pickup swerved as the driver slammed on the brakes and veered sharply into the driveway. The rear of the truck partly blocked her path. She blindly hit her door locks and rolled up her windows, her heart in her throat, as she stared at the burly, late-middle-aged man behind the wheel.

He shoved open the driver's-side door, stepped outside and stalked over to her window, where he leered at her, his fleshy lips parted to expose tobacco-stained teeth.

He signaled her to roll down her window, but she shook her head and fumbled for the cell phone she'd laid on the seat of the truck.

"You know you can't get away with this," he growled, his voice muffled through the glass.

The dogs in the back of her truck had been quiet, but now they set up a round of crazed barking that drowned out the rest of his words.

She shrugged, waving a hand at her ear, and mouthed the word, "Sorry."

His face deepened to a dark red. "You'll be hearing from my lawyers—mark my words," he shouted. "And you'll be begging to apologize. Begging on your *knees*—did you hear me?"

The noise of the dogs scrambling around in their cages and their frantic barking rose to an explosion of fear.

She motioned with both palms up, then gripped the steering wheel and eased around his battered pickup, careful to avoid his bumper and the mailbox. Glancing quickly to the right and left, she pulled out onto the highway and stepped on the gas, her heart beating madly against her ribs.

Court orders and assistance from the sheriff's department or not, Bascomb wasn't happy, and he wasn't just going to let this go. She could feel it in her bones. And meeting him again on his own, secluded turf— or anywhere else—was the last thing she wanted to do.

What had she gotten herself into?

Trace shook some slack out in the reins and nudged the colt into a lope, forcing himself to concentrate on the gelding's easy three-beat cadence and headset as they traversed the indoor arena from one end to the other.

His thoughts still kept veering back to Wind Hill Ranch.

He had plenty to do at home: several two-year-olds that he was just starting under saddle. And older horses that he'd been training for cutting and reining performance classes next summer.

Foaling and calving plus the usual chores that kept him busy from dawn until dusk no matter what the season. With the changeable March weather, feeding livestock could mean being buried in mud one day and tromping through snow the next. It was enough to keep a man's mind busy, just staying ahead of everything…

Except for his recurrent thoughts about the blonde at the neighboring ranch, who had clearly tackled more than she could handle with her fool idea about running an animal shelter…and the pervading sense of unease that filled his thoughts whenever his mind wandered back to her.

He'd been so careful to avoid emotional entanglements during the years since the accident at the Denver rodeo. The thought of complications and responsibility for someone else made his blood run cold. Sure, Carrie was here at the ranch now, but she was spunky and independent and had her own life as a teacher… and woe to anyone who got in her way if she was on a mission to help someone.

Kris Donaldson was another story.

She was a woman who needed protecting, but he wasn't the man for the job. Even if he ever could finally come to peace within himself over his failures, how could anyone else?

Yet he couldn't get her out of his mind. And it made him…edgy, somehow, though his lingering feeling that she could be in trouble was crazy. He'd *seen* some of the traffic pulling into her lane when he drove past on his way to Lost Falls yesterday, and she sure didn't lack company. With all those people around, how could anything go wrong?

Carrie appeared at the far end of the arena and waved to him, so he settled the colt into a walk and headed over to her.

"Nice," Carrie said, smiling up at him when he pulled to a stop next to her. "He's coming along really well."

"Shows promise."

Her eyebrows drew together as she canted her head and studied him for a minute. "Something wrong?"

"Nope."

"You seem…distracted."

He shrugged. "Just tired. There was a fire call last night, and we didn't finish up until almost four."

"Anyone we know?" Her voice filled with worry. "Was anyone hurt?"

"No, thank goodness. It was an abandoned house out in the country, on the other side of town."

"Were you able to figure out the cause?"

"Too dark last night, but I went back this morning

and sifted through the debris. There weren't any scents of accelerant or the typical char pattern for that type of arson. It looks like the fire started in a rusted wood stove. Accidental, not arson."

"But someone must've been there."

"I'm guessing some teenagers were having a little party, or maybe a vagrant was holed up there. There was quite a pile of beer cans inside."

Carrie shook her head. "What a shame. Some historic old home…."

He laughed. "A crumbling shack of a house at best."

"Still." She pursed her lips and gazed across the arena at a pair of cats chasing each other in circles, and then he knew she hadn't just idly stopped by. "Since you're tired and all, maybe you could use a break."

He rested a forearm on the saddle horn and waited.

"I got busy with lesson plans and grading papers, and haven't been over to see Kris for a while. Don't you think we ought to go over and say hi?"

"I was just there on Wednesday."

"Really." Her eyes twinkled. "That's good to hear."

He stifled a groan at her transparent delight. "So you can go on over and visit awhile. I need to stay here and work these horses or they'll forget everything they ever knew."

"Please?"

She was an eternal optimist, but she was wasting her breath if she thought she could play matchmaker and fix his life. He reined the colt toward the center of the arena. "Sorry."

"You work too hard, Trace," she pleaded. "You've got to slow down. At least let that investigator job go."

"I can't. You know why." But even as he cued the colt into an easy jog, the hint of worry in her voice hit him square in the gut. Things hadn't been easy for her lately, either. The least he could do was try to be fair.

"Maybe tomorrow?" He glanced over his shoulder at her and saw a hint of a smile.

"I'm taking dinner over there. Today." Her soft voice drifted across the ring like a siren's song. "Fried chicken…red potato salad…coconut cake. *And I'm leaving the leftovers there.*"

At a slight lift of the reins, the colt dropped into a neat sliding stop. Trace shifted his weight, and the animal executed a 180-degree turn to face Carrie.

"Coconut cake?"

"Gooey seven-minute frosting with loads of toasted coconut. Three layers."

The vision of supper heading over to the neighboring ranch, leaving canned soup and sandwiches as Trace's usual fallback plan, made the decision a little easier. After all, he could simply view Kris Donaldson as another pesky sister, and it would make things easier for everyone.

Already knowing his answer, Carrie turned toward the house, her fingertips raised in fluttery farewell. "I'm leaving in an hour."

"Maybe she won't be home."

"Don't count on it, cowboy. Whether you like it or not, we're gonna *socialize.*"

* * *

Veterinarian Gina Lang looked up from the emaciated dog she'd just finished examining. "Have you heard from the owner yet?"

"Not a word. The sheriff says he hasn't heard from the Bascombs either, so he stopped by their place and it looked empty, so maybe they left town. Honestly, I'm glad. I hope they just stay away and don't fight the county on this. I'd love to re-home every one of these poor dogs and give them a decent life."

The veterinarian gently ran her hand over the knobs of the dog's spine. "I'm with you a hundred percent. Believe it or not, the Bascombs were once well-known in this region for their champion field-trial dogs, but that was a while ago."

"If this is how they cared for their dogs, I can hardly believe it."

"Harvey is—or was—a certified field-trial judge, and his dogs were once high in the regional standings. I understand he's had some considerable problems, though."

Kris held her hands out in frustration. "Nothing that could warrant *this*."

"I don't like gossip." Gina hesitated. "But I guess it's common knowledge because most of it was in the court reports section of the paper. There were some domestic abuse and DWI charges, then his wife divorced him. There were also some legal issues involving the sale of several dogs. Not, mind you, that any of that is an excuse for neglect. Maybe he got in so far over his head that he just didn't care anymore." Gina held the dog's head gently between her hands and peered into its eyes. "You're a good boy, aren't you? You'll be feeling better in no time."

"He's the last one for you to see today. Thanks so much for coming out." Kris took the leash and led the dog out of the examination area of the kennel office and back to his pen. "Can you send the county a bill and send me a copy, too?"

"You bet." Gina turned to the counter and began gathering her supplies. "I'll leave you bandaging materials and antibiotics that ought to hold you for a few days. Can you stop by the clinic to pick up the rest?"

"Absolutely."

She looked at her watch. "Guess I'd better run. I have a few more calls, and then the kids from the church preschool are coming to the clinic for a tour." She grinned. "I love it when they come. Everyone is absolutely thrilled."

From outside came the sound of a truck pulling to a stop.

Bailey, who had been curled up on his bed in the corner of the office for the past hour, raised his head for a single, welcoming woof.

"That has to be a truck from the Rocking R," Kris said with a laugh. "He's much more energetic if he doesn't recognize the vehicle."

Gina hesitated and looked back, her hand on the doorknob. "You've met Trace and Carrie?"

"They've been over several times. Nice people."

"They go to the Community Church here in town. Carrie lights up the place like fireworks when she gets excited about something. She just took over the Sunday School program, and she really has people revved up. Everyone just loves her."

"And...Trace?"

"A great guy. I'm glad he's back in town."

"Carrie and I have hit it off pretty well, but I think Trace wishes I'd never shown up here. He's so... distant."

Gina nodded. "He's quiet, but then, with all that happened...well, it hasn't been easy."

Kris felt her heart catch. "What?"

Gina's cheeks colored. "I guess you'd better ask him or Carrie. It isn't my place to say."

NINE

Kris watched Gina go outside and talk to Trace and Carrie, then she turned back to check all of the dog runs, looking in on each animal as she went down the line.

Even after just two days of adequate food, fresh water and warm, clean housing, the Bascomb dogs seemed to be looking a little perkier, though the vet had said it might take a month or more of care before some of the pressure sores would heal.

Yesterday, Kris had worked her way through the entire pack, bathing them and gently cleansing wounds. Not one of them had tried to snap at her, perhaps realizing that she was only trying to help. She'd been near tears over some of them—the young ones who feared her touch. The old ones, too weak to care.

Today she felt a sense of deep contentment just walking past and seeing their eyes were a little brighter. Satisfied that all was well, she left the building and went out to meet the Randalls.

Carrie waved gaily and turned to pull a large picnic basket out of the backseat of the truck. She thrust it into Trace's arms, then retrieved a large plastic container and pushed the door shut.

"Tell me that you haven't eaten lunch yet," she called out. "I have enough for an army here, and Gina couldn't stay."

The aromas drifting on the light breeze made Kris's mouth water. "It smells heavenly. And no. I haven't eaten—not even breakfast. We had quite a morning, once the vet arrived."

She followed Carrie and Trace into the kitchen, where Carrie began reaching into the basket and pulling out a nine-by-thirteen pan heaped with chicken and covered with aluminum foil, followed by several serving dishes. She put them all in the center of the round oak table in the kitchen.

"I figured you don't have much time to cook these days, and it was time for us to be neighborly." Carrie grinned at her brother. "We can't stay too awfully long, though, 'cause Trace has his hands full back at the ranch. It was the coconut cake that lured him here."

The laugh lines bracketing his eyes deepened. "That sounds pathetic."

She nodded. "He is, actually, when it comes to this cake and my fried chicken."

"I don't blame him a bit." Kris pulled plates and silverware from the cupboards and set them on the table, then pulled a pitcher of iced tea from the refrigerator. "I hope this'll do."

"Perfect. Can we say grace?" Carrie reached out to hold hands.

Kris accepted the gesture, then tentatively reached for Trace, suddenly feeling a little shy and awkward. His hand was large and strong and calloused. Little shimmers of awareness made her own hand tingle and sent a rush of warmth through her. Their eyes met for a split second, then he bowed his head.

But in that brief moment, she saw something beyond the casual, indifferent expression he usually wore. Was that really a flash of…*interest?*

Carrie closed her eyes. "Dear Lord, thanks so much for bringing Kris into our lives. Please bless her work here and help her prosper while caring for all of Your creatures in need. Please keep her safe and well, and help her find happiness in our midst. Please bless Trace in all he does, and keep us all safe. Thank You for this food and for all the joy and love You have brought us. Amen."

"Amen."

Trace's husky voice rumbled across Kris's skin and she pulled her hand back, a little too quickly.

"Well, dig in," Carrie urged. "This is family-style, and we sure don't stand on formality."

The chicken was incredible—juicy, plump and well seasoned with a wonderful crispy coating. The potato salad held a hint of dill, garlic and sour cream, unlike any other recipe Kris had tried.

Throughout the meal, she mostly sat back and listened to the easy banter between Trace and his sister.

"This was just amazing," she murmured when she couldn't eat another bite. "And your dinner rolls—they're light as a cloud. Whenever I've tried, I end up with doorstops."

Carrie laughed. "Practice, my dear. That's all it takes…along with too many failures to count."

"Though even your failures beat my best, six ways to Sunday," Trace retorted. "And that…well, that's the best thing this side of heaven."

He leaned back in his chair and looked longingly at the tall plastic cake container on the counter, looking so boyish that it made Kris smile.

Taking the hint, she rose to clear the plates and dishes from the table, while Carrie uncovered the cake and cut it into thick slabs.

He was right—Carrie's cake was well beyond delicious.

"How are things going for you over here?" he asked after polishing off the last crumb. "Busy?"

Kris toyed with her fork, wishing she had enough appetite to finish her serving. "The kennel is full right now. A couple dozen animals are here after a seizure due to neglect and are essentially impounded for the next thirty days. Otherwise, word is starting to spread. There've been four canine adoptions and three kittens so far…but more keep coming in."

"Any…trouble?"

Carrie looked up from her cake, her gaze darting between them. "Trouble?"

"Nothing, really. Trace saw some footprints up on

the hill, but they were just from some hiker. Or someone coming out for some nature photography."

Allan's phone call still haunted her; still made her wonder if he could have told his buddies about her location. But surely, if they were free now, they wouldn't risk that freedom for revenge.

"You don't *look* like everything is all right." Carrie studied her face. "You look worried. Is there anything we can do?"

"I'm good. Really. Between all the dogs barking and the security system at the house, no one could sneak in here. And Trace has told me I can call him if I'm ever uneasy."

"I sure hope you do." Trace shoved away from the table and headed for the door. "I'm going to take a walk around the buildings. Can we be ready to go in maybe twenty minutes?"

Carrie nodded, then rose and began putting the leftovers into the refrigerator. "This'll keep you in meals for a couple days." She grinned and nudged Kris with her elbow as she wrapped the foil around the remaining chicken. "The cake might even bring Trace back over for another visit, and then you can put him to work."

"I couldn't. I mean…"

"Are you *blushing?*" Carrie wiggled an eyebrow.

"Of course not. I mean, he's been a good neighbor, but…"

"Well, for the record, I think you two would be a great couple. And," Carrie added with a mischievous smile, "I think I'm gonna tell him."

If Kris hadn't been blushing before, she surely was now. She could feel the heat climbing up her neck. "Please don't. I get the feeling he can't wait to escape, whenever he's over here." She hesitated. "I'm curious, though. The vet said something about him having troubles, in the past."

Carrie abruptly turned away to search under the kitchen sink, and pulled out a bottle of dish detergent. "You…should probably ask him."

"That's what Gina said. I hope I haven't inadvertently said something wrong to him."

Carrie closed the sink drain and poured in some detergent, then started running the hot water. After a moment she shut off the faucet and turned around. "Trace…wouldn't like me talking about him. You should let him tell you, when he's ready. But I can say this—he's a man who shoulders responsibility too heavily. I wish I could lift his burdens, but I can't— and that's just something he and God need to work out someday. God is always ready to forgive…but it's Trace who just can't forgive himself."

Kris mulled over Carrie's words after the Randalls left. What on earth would trouble Trace so much that he couldn't forgive himself?

Her cell phone rang just as she reached the kennel. Her heart skipped a beat—then settled into a steadier rhythm when she saw Megan's name on the screen.

"Sorry I didn't get back to you sooner. I've been working overtime." Something crackled in the background—probably her patrol car radio—and she fell silent for a moment before continuing, her voice weary. "How are things?"

"You sound swamped, Meg."

"That and more, but I wouldn't do this if I didn't love it. Have you heard from Allan since we last met?"

"No…"

After a pause, Megan sighed. "You didn't give him any money. Please tell me you didn't."

"I'm not stupid. But he said he knew something about Emma. So, yeah…I sent him a little."

"And then you learned all about your sister. After all these years."

"Well, no…but he did have some information he could only have gotten from her. And he said he wouldn't keep track of her if I didn't help him."

"He knows your hot buttons, sweetie. He knows less about Emma than even you do—I can guarantee it. He probably just recited something you said about her years ago. He's nothing if not smart—but he only uses those brain cells to find an easy way through life."

"That's exactly what *my* brain tells me. It's just that sometimes, my heart gets in the way. Emma means everything to me. She's the only relative I have left." Again, Kris heard a burst of static in the background. "Are you okay?"

"I have to go. But I want to tell you that Allan's buddies are definitely out on parole. They've both failed recent meetings with their parole officers, so now they're under warrants for arrest. No one has seen them for several months."

A shudder worked its way through Kris's midsection. "Not what I wanted to hear."

"They'd be stupid to come after you, but no one said *all* criminals are smart. I want you to talk to your local sheriff and give him the details. Got that? And do it now. The local agencies need to know that you were once threatened by these guys, so they can be on alert. I—oops, gotta go."

The line went dead.

Kris debated, then called the sheriff's office and left a message, though it didn't seem plausible that Jay and Tom would come clear over to Montana to retaliate. Her testimony during their trial was still safely stored in old court records. It would provide an obvious link. And surely the last thing they'd want was to risk capture and end up back in the slammer. But, if she hadn't followed through, Megan would've hounded her relentlessly until she did.

The rest of the day flew by. A family arrived for a joyous reunion with their missing cocker spaniel—a dog the sheriff had brought in yesterday after he found it wandering far out in the country.

Another owner arrived, relieved to find his missing coonhound, but he became testy about the forty-dollar charge to get it back.

And—something that made her smile during the late afternoon—she looked out the window by her desk in the office and saw a familiar minivan pull in with three small girls and their clearly embarrassed father.

After their last visit, Kris had worried about how he treated his family, but as he walked to the building, the girls held his hands while they skipped and chattered excitedly. *Good.*

As soon as he opened the door, the girls ran down the aisle to look for their favorite calico kitten, but he lingered in front of her desk, his hands shoved in his pockets, until Kris looked up from the papers on her desk. "Yes?"

"I…uh…guess I need to apologize." His face was the picture of contrition, and he could barely look her in the eye. "I was a little rude when we were here a few days ago. My wife hasn't been speaking to me and the girls have been crying ever since over the kitten they wanted. Is…is it still here?"

"I believe so."

"Thank God." His shoulders slumped with obvious relief. "All three girls have been adding this onto their bedtime prayers for days."

She tried to hide her smile. "If you want you can go out to see her, to make sure it's the right decision, then you can sign the adoption application. There's a four-day wait after that, or you can wait another week and the kitten would be spayed here."

"I promise we'll follow through, but for any peace at our house, I'd sure like to pick her up as soon as we can."

"No problem." Kris swiveled her chair and retrieved a folder from the cabinet behind her desk. "I'll definitely hold that kitten for you—but the four days start once you fill this out, so you might want to do it now." She glanced at the calendar. "Then you could come back on…Tuesday."

"Again—I'm sorry." He ventured a tentative smile. "I'd had a hard day at work, and I took it out on you. My wife wasted no time in letting me know what she thought of me."

Little feet came thundering back down the aisle, then his three girls burst into the office, grinning from ear to ear.

"She's *here,* Daddy!"

"Please, can we have her? Please?"

The older girl's eyes sparkled with tears. "It's the one, Daddy. It's the right one."

They gathered around him, hugging his waist, and burst into childish cheers when he said yes.

Those children and their father weren't far from Kris's thoughts late on Sunday evening, while she sat on the floor and tackled yet another box of Thalia's possessions that were still stacked in the living room.

Those sweet little faces.

Their excitement.

Their complete adoration and forgiveness of their father, even if he'd been abominably rude.

What was it like to experience such complete and forgiving love? To be the most important person in a small child's life? She caught her reflection in the windows as she took a pile of linens to the back door to be donated and stopped short.

She was still young. There were still possibilities for her out there…but the person looking back at her in reflection looked grim. Tired. Older than her years.

The polar opposite of perky little Carrie, who seemed to face each day with boundless joy and energy.

Remembering the easy banter between Carrie and her brother, Kris felt a flash of longing for the camaraderie she would likely never have. With her own sister gone and one failed marriage under her belt, she was probably destined to end up as a loony old lady living alone with twenty cats and a parakeet.

Despite the senseless fluttering of those butterflies in her stomach when Trace showed up, guys like him didn't settle for women with a lot of baggage…or the kind of secrets she didn't want to reveal.

And women like her knew it wasn't worth the risk of even trying…because it just meant facing an inevitable sense of loss.

Lost in her thoughts, she started on another box…then froze as she lifted her gaze to the windows. It was pitch-black outside. Way after midnight.

And outside, the dogs in the kennel were going absolutely crazy.

TEN

When the furious barking out in the kennel rose to an even higher crescendo, Kris realized three things.

The dogs heard wildlife coming into the clearing, or they sensed a two-footed predator.

And the only weapon she had—Thalia's Winchester—was in the kennel and far out of reach.

Her heart pounding, she slowly rose to her knees, then moved to the kitchen, where the lights were off and she'd be less easily seen.

The single security light cast a pool of light over the front door of the main entrance to the kennels, fading to darkness at either end.

Through the window of the office she could see the glow of the single light she always left on inside.

Nothing was moving. Yet the dogs suddenly grew louder, and far more frantic.

And then she saw it—a dim, crouching shadow moving along the side of the building, just outside the pool of light. Animal…or *human?*

Her heart jerked upward into her throat, making it hard to breathe. To think.

Rushing out there would be stupid. Unarmed, defenseless, she would be an easy target...or easy prey. *But what if something—or someone—was after the dogs, trapped?*

Yet if she called 911 or Trace and it was nothing but a random coyote or wolf, she'd seem like some hysterical, ridiculous woman who couldn't handle running the shelter on her own...news that could well spread from the sheriff to the county board of supervisors and endanger her provisional contract.

Unclipping the cell phone at her waist, she waited. Strained to listen past the howling erupting from the kennel. Toenails clicked across the kitchen floor and Bailey shoved his nose under her hand, whining. He went to the back door, whined, and came back to her, edgy and uncertain.

But the old dog was no match for a wolf, much less a pack if one was near. "Not this time, buddy."

God—I don't talk to You near enough, but I'm begging You now. Please—tell me what to do.

Whatever the damage to her credibility, she had to call.

With shaking fingers she punched in 911, then gave her name to the dispatcher. "I hear something outside. The dogs are going berserk, and I'm unarmed."

"Kris Donaldson?" he asked after a brief pause. "This number is coming up as out-of-state."

"It's my cell. I'm living at Wind Hill Ranch, west of Battle Creek."

"Have you seen an intruder? Have you been directly threatened?"

"No…but someone, or something, is out there."

A brief silence. "Officer Gardner is within a few miles of your location. He's on his way. Stay on the line, ma'am. Tell me what you're seeing now."

Kris spoke rapidly into the phone, keeping her eyes fixed on the murky landscape outside. After what seemed like a lifetime, a pair of headlights briefly twinkled through the trees along the lane coming from the highway, then came bouncing into view.

The patrol car pulled in and did a slow circle in the parking area, its spotlight scanning the entire clearing, and then the buildings from one end to another.

The tenor of the barking changed, then quieted altogether when the patrol car halted under the light by the house.

Kris ended her 911 call and moved to the front entryway, waiting until she saw Ken's familiar bulk climbing out of the car. She opened the door.

"Sorry about this," she called out.

He smiled as he trudged up the porch steps. "It's my job, ma'am. Did you see someone?"

"The dogs have been going crazy. I saw a shadow moving out there, but it disappeared before you got here. Could've been a person crouched low…maybe even an animal. I just couldn't tell, and it seemed foolish to go out there unarmed, just in case."

"Absolutely right. I didn't see anything, and all of the windows and doors appear to be shut tight, but that doesn't mean that there wasn't good reason to call."

She crossed her arms over her chest and rubbed her upper arms. "Have there been any break-ins in the area lately?"

"Nope. No sighting of wolves, either, though a pack does run in the area. They're as elusive as can be, so you might never see them." He glanced around her kitchen. "Everything good up here at the house?"

"No problems. Everything is locked tight, and I do have a security system in place."

"Good, good." He grasped his service belt and adjusted its bulk. "I'm going out to check the building a little closer. You stay here."

"Can I ask you a question first?"

"Fire away."

"With the things going on here, I just want to know. Carrie said Thalia's death was accidental. Is that true?"

"We found absolutely no evidence to the contrary."

"Well, that's a relief."

"The best we could figure was that fog was rising up out of the ravines that morning." He shook his head and sighed with obvious regret. "The morning started off cool and damp, then the temperatures dropped. Thalia probably got confused in the mist, then hit an icy patch. A terrible accident, but that's it. End of story."

"No foul play."

"Thalia was the least likely target of anyone you could ever think of. She had no expensive electronics to steal, she wasn't rich. No enemies or rivals. No family or romantic entanglements. No one tried to buy up her property after she died, so there wasn't anyone coveting her home. Sometimes, no matter what people want to believe, accidents do happen."

"I suppose so."

He looked over his shoulder at the outbuildings. "The dogs are quiet, so I'd guess the intruder—whatever it was—is gone. I'll just go on ahead and look things over. Be back in a minute."

She watched him walk out to the cruiser and climb in, then take another slow circuit around the plowed areas by the buildings. At the kennel, he got out from behind the wheel and walked along the building holding a big flashlight in one hand, his other hand resting loosely on his holstered service revolver.

Then he went inside, and she saw all of the lights flare on. A few minutes later the lights went off and he emerged from the door. She sighed with relief.

When he came back into the house, he had Thalia's rifle in hand. "If those dogs were raising a big ruckus, I'd guess they smelled wolves or bear. You might want to keep this handy. It would certainly stop a human or a coyote, though I don't think this model would do more than irritate a charging grizzly."

She managed a weak smile. "Something I'd definitely rather not do."

"Nope. Male grizzlies tend to come out of hibernation mid to late March, and we've already had some sightings. Black bears wake up a little later."

"Grumpy, I'll bet."

"Sure 'nuff. But just seeing one doesn't mean you should shoot. There's a limited season, and you need a permit—unless you've got one endangering livestock or human life." He put Thalia's rifle on the counter. "I use a .32 Remington myself, or a .30-30. But for now, at least you have this."

"Do you think we had a bear out there?"

"There've been so many people tramping through the snow around the buildings that I can't make out any new footprints in this light. Some of your little visitors have been romping in the snow clear out to the fences, and there are lots of dog tracks out there, too."

"I tell people to go outside with their prospective pets, to get acquainted."

"Either Sam or I will stop out tomorrow and search the perimeter of the clearing for any tracks leading in. I'm guessing you did have a bear. Maybe it was lured by the scent of pet food and your trash cans but ran off before it could get into trouble. If one starts hanging around too close, we might need to call in the DNR for a relocation."

"I can go out and check myself, come morning."

"We'll be back." He met and held her gaze. "My headlights probably scared off whatever was out there. Maybe it wasn't really a serious threat. But if the dogs were going crazy, you were right in calling for help. Don't ever hesitate to do that, understand? It's when people are too brave, too reckless, that a situation can go south in a hurry."

* * *

Kris parked at the far edge of the Battle Creek Community Church parking lot and took a deep breath to calm her nerves. Then she stepped out of her SUV and joined the last stragglers who were heading through the big oak double doors.

Some of her foster homes had been judgmental and strict. Some completely lax. Only a few had made church a strong part of their lives. With that patchwork beginning, she'd only intermittently attended and the places of worship were constantly changing, though while at the Parkers', she'd managed to stay long enough to be confirmed.

Without strong roots, she'd drifted away as an adult.

But ever since coming to Battle Creek, a still, small voice in her heart had been urging her to make the connection again. Whether because of Carrie's clear, strong faith or because she was completely on her own in uncharted waters, she'd thought about church every Sunday…then found an excuse to not go.

Would people stare? Ask uncomfortable questions? Even after a childhood filled with a series of family and ever changing schools, that chilling, self-conscious moment of stepping into a new place as an outsider still made her stomach clench.

She moved out of the bright sunlight and through the doors. Inside, the air had a different feel—scented by wood polish, burning candles and flowers, the light warmed by the sunshine streaming through the tall stained-glass windows in the sanctuary ahead.

When her eyes adjusted, she realized that an elderly, overweight woman stood to her right, her face wreathed in a gentle smile, her hand extended.

"Hello, dearie. So glad you're here." She leaned forward with a conspiratorial wink. "Don't forget the coffee hour afterward. I brought a pan of my pecan caramel rolls—so you'll want to get in line quick or they'll be gone. Especially if my grandson gets at 'em first."

The woman was all silver hair, wrinkles and softness, like the grandmother Kris had never had, and she felt a tug of longing in her heart. Family. Lifelong friends. The tightly woven relationships of a small town, where everyone knew everyone else and even knew what their best friend's sister's boyfriend had done in second grade. Connections that went deep.

If she stayed here for good, would she ever become a part of that fabric? Was it even possible?

She accepted a bulletin from the usher standing at the door of the sanctuary, scanned the pews uncertainly, then slipped into an empty one just a few rows up.

The back of her neck prickled, and she knew people were staring at this stranger in their midst. Uncomfortable, she slipped a little lower in her seat.

A moment later, someone slid in next to her…and then several others, too, until she'd had to slide halfway down the long pew.

The person next to her leaned close and jostled her shoulder. "Hey!"

Startled by the familiar voice, she lifted her frozen gaze from the bulletin in her hands. *"Carrie?"*

"And Trace and our grandma Betsy," Carrie whispered. "Trace and I had some loose calves to catch, so we're a little late. Grandma, however, has never been late for anything in her life."

Kris leaned forward and found Trace sitting next to his sister. She nodded at him, feeling a little rush of pleasure as she took in his thick dark hair—for once, without a Stetson covering it—and his black leather blazer and pressed jeans.

He nodded, then tipped his head to his other side where Kris found the sweet old woman from the doorway beaming at her. She hid a grin, realizing that Trace was probably the caramel roll addict.

No longer feeling as conspicuous and alone, Kris settled back in her seat. Prisms of jewel-colored light sparkled in the windows, casting a soft glow over the congregation. An organist up in the loft began to play "Beautiful Savior," and she felt a warm, gentle sense of peace flood through her.

She'd felt a moment of tension, walking through the doors, but this place wasn't vibrating with the harsh judgment she'd felt—or perhaps just imagined—as a child.

A few pews ahead, she noticed familiar faces... Ray, the Kitten Man, with his wife and three little girls. An elderly gentleman who had come to the shelter in tears to leave his beloved old Brittany spaniel, Lucy, because he was growing too frail to care for her. A dog that would stay with Kris for the rest of its days unless she found the perfect forever home.

Farther up, Deputy Ken Gardner and Polly and others whom Kris had seen in town. And—her heart took an extra beat. *Erin?* Her old childhood friend? She was sitting with a handsome man and a young boy, her arm draped around the child's shoulders as she bent down to whisper something in his ear. She looked so content, so happy, that Kris smiled to herself.

Apparently life had been good to her.

After the liturgy and several hymns, the pastor moved to the pulpit. Surprisingly young, he exuded enthusiasm and warmth as he smiled and read the lesson from the twenty-third Psalm. *"Even though I walk through the valley of the shadow of death, I will fear no evil, for you are with me; your rod and your staff, they comfort me…"*

Her thoughts slipped back to Laura's death. For years, she'd been so angry, so devastated. So overwhelmed with the injustice of it all. A child herself, she'd been angry with God for allowing her friend to die. Her own faith had faltered amidst the fear that God wouldn't protect her from the monsters in the night, either.

In time she'd understood, at least on an intellectual level. Bad things *could* happen to innocent people. It wasn't punishment or heavenly retribution. It was just the vagaries of nature, the evil of men and their freedom of choice. Sheer physics, like Thalia falling from that mountain trail.

Maybe there were no promises of safety and happiness and good health, but she felt a deeper sense of peace slip around her heart—as if God held it in His loving hands and promised to be with her, no matter what life brought her way.

Both deputies had stopped by on Tuesday morning to search for bear tracks. They'd walked around the perimeter of the property, but found nothing more than countless footprints, probably all from shelter visitors. Some of them trailed off into government land, but then she'd seen plenty of kids playing tag and straying far over the fences while their parents were mulling over adoption forms, so that didn't mean anything.

But knowing there hadn't been a bear close by didn't make her feel any safer. Instead, her uneasiness had grown with each passing night. Was someone still out there, roaming the woods? Watching and waiting?

For what?

The message in today's sermon was the kind of reassurance she needed more than ever. She only hoped it could help calm her racing heart once night fell and the dogs started barking again.

ELEVEN

On Monday, Carrie sent Trace over with a meat loaf, creamy garlic mashed potatoes and French silk frosted brownies because she'd "inadvertently" made too much for just Trace and herself. On Tuesday, she sent him over with a large stack of newspapers for a pen of abandoned puppies that had come into the shelter the night before.

On Wednesday, he arrived in the late afternoon with a load of dry cat and dog food that had been left in the donation box at the feed store in town…again, at Carrie's request.

"I'm afraid," he said with a weary laugh, "that Carrie is on a mission."

Kris smiled back at him, thankful that they'd finally become more comfortable with each other. And who wouldn't be, after fighting over the last incredible caramel roll at church last Sunday? They'd ended up sharing it, of course, under his grandmother's watchful eye…with Carrie laughing and insisting that it was actually hers.

The speculative looks Carrie directed between Kris and Trace as they all finished their coffee had been a definite hint of what was to come.

"She's one of the most delightful people I know."

"And the most determined." He hefted the last bag of dog kibble from the back of his truck to the waiting wheelbarrow, then leaned against the open tailgate. "We could drive her mad, by completely ignoring her ploys."

"That would do it, I think."

"Or we could go out for dinner just once and make her a happy woman."

A little rush of anticipation made Kris feel giddy. How long had it been since she'd actually been out for an evening with a nice, attractive guy? She couldn't even remember. "I suppose that depends on how much you want to pay her back for all of these errands."

"Good point." He gazed out across the meadow, where four inches of new snow had turned drab grass and dirty, melting snowdrifts back into a pristine wonderland. "So what do you think?" When she didn't answer right away, he looked back at her, his eyes dark and gentle, quietly waiting.

"If that's an invitation to dinner, then I guess we ought to make Carrie happy."

"Saturday—say, eight o'clock?"

"It's a deal."

Kris followed him as he pushed away from the tailgate, moved the dog food into the storeroom, then propped the wheelbarrow against the wall and closed the door.

All up and down the aisle, a chorus of dogs yelped and barked and jumped at the front of their cages, vying for attention as they walked past.

"Thanks for all your help. And the meat loaf. And the newspapers." She bit her lower lip. "But if something comes up…or you have second thoughts about Saturday, just let me know. I'll be cool either way."

He hesitated at the door. Bowed his head, then turned to face her with a faint smile that didn't quite reach his eyes. "I'll be here, though maybe you should be the one to call it off."

The prospect of going on a date made Kris feel she was once again a giddy, unpolished girl of seventeen. What *did* people wear on a date, these days? There were swanky supper clubs open during tourist season, but off-season those were surely closed.

Casual slacks? Dressy?

A basic little black dress?

Did she have anything that even came close? Probably not.

Recalling a little consignment shop tucked between a pizza parlor and barbershop on the main drag through town, she put a "back in two hours" sign on the kennel door and headed into Battle Creek, praying that the store hadn't been a figment of her imagination. And that it was open.

Off-season many of the businesses had limited hours. Some were closed on certain days. She held her breath as she pulled to a stop in front, then heaved a sigh of relief at the open sign in the window.

Inside circular racks were crammed with clothing, as were the racks lining each wall. A bored thirtysomething brunette looked up from polishing her nails at the register.

"Looking for something special?"

"Just…something for church. Or maybe an evening dinner out."

The woman offered a vague wave of her hand. "Racks are set up by size. Take your pick. Fitting rooms are in the back. If you need any help, I'm Janet. Oh—and the pink tags are fifty percent off."

At least she wasn't going to hover.

Kris worked her way through the possibilities, holding first one outfit and then another in front of herself at the big mirror on the wall.

Too formal.

Too flouncy.

Too I'm-so-desperate.

Too I'm-over-the-hill and out-of-date.

With a sigh, she put each of them back, then gathered others until she couldn't stand another minute of frustration. On her way to the door she stopped. "What about this outfit on the mannequin? Is it for sale?"

"*Everything's* for sale in here. You want it, it's yours."

Kris studied the ivory silk slacks and matching pullover sweater for a long moment, then caressed the soft weave of the sweater. It looked comfortable.

Elegant. Adult without being dowdy. It probably cost the earth.

"How much?"

The clerk blew at her nails without looking up. "Check the sticker underneath the label."

It read fifty dollars…but the tag was pink.

Feeling as if she'd just embarked on a treasure hunt, Kris carefully slipped the garments off the mannequin and tried them on in the dressing room.

With her blond hair and pale ivory skin, she'd never thought she could pull off a such a light, neutral color, but this shade and fabric seemed to make her skin glow, while bringing up the highlights in her hair.

"I'll take it," she called out, feeling girlish and extravagant all at once.

At the cash register, she carefully folded the clothing and set it on the counter, then pulled her checkbook out, her pen poised while the clerk figured out the total with tax.

The woman's gaze slid over the blank check, her neck craning around to read Kris's name upside down. "You're the gal who's out at the animal shelter."

Kris smiled at her. "That's right."

A ruddy wash of color crawled up the woman's neck. "I…uh…can only take cash."

"But…what about this sign?" Right on the counter, taped to the glass, a green square of paper announced that any returned checks would incur a $50.00 penalty by the store, plus any other charges by the bank.

"Cash, ma'am." The woman's voice held a thread of steel. "Only cash."

"I don't understand."

"Look, I don't want trouble. I just can't afford bad checks or bad credit cards. If you've got the money, you can go on down to the bank and get some cash, but I can't afford to lose out." Her gaze skated away and her blush deepened. "I…I changed my policy this month. Guess I just didn't get the sign down."

Embarrassment flooded through Kris at the implication that she was a bad risk.

"It's okay," she said, keeping her voice gentle. "I do have some cash in my purse…but can you tell me why you're concerned?"

"Policy. Just—policy."

Kris pulled a twenty and a ten out of her billfold and handed it to her. After she had the receipt, change and her purchase in hand, she tried again. "Please? I just need to know."

The clerk's lips compressed into a hard line. "It couldn't stay a secret long, you know. Not in a good town like this…with decent, hard-working folks."

"Secret?" Even to her own ears, her voice sounded hollow.

"About your bad debts and legal troubles." She almost spat the words. "And drug charges—but you got off of them because of that pretty face."

Kris stared at her, stunned and speechless.

"Like I said, we don't want trouble around here…and I hope the sheriff is watching you close."

She'd paid for her mistakes in the past. Ever since then, she'd worked so hard to turn her life around. To be a responsible, law-abiding citizen. Yet a reputation was such a fragile thing—so easily destroyed. Had Allan managed to spread his lies here? No matter how much she denied them, rumors could fly like the wind, and this wasn't the first time he'd subtly tried to ruin her.

"Where did you hear all that?"

The woman eyed her with suspicion. "You might think this place is backwoods, but that doesn't mean the truth don't get around."

"Look, my ex-husband was once in a lot of trouble, and I fell into that world for a while, but that happened many years ago. My word is good and my checks are, too. Just ask at the bank."

"Maybe…"

"The sheriff is welcome to do a background check on me anytime. In fact, I imagine he did, before I got to open the animal shelter." Kris's shock had grown into anger, and now she took a slow, steadying breath. "Have you never, ever done something you wished you could change? Or found yourself the target of malicious gossip? Please—go talk to him, before you pass judgment. These rumors could ruin my life here."

The woman dropped her gaze.

"And do consider," Kris added gently, "that anyone passing it along could be sued for slander. I wonder who else in town is guilty of that? I'd like to know."

* * *

Out in her SUV, Kris started the engine, then draped her shaking hands over the top of the steering wheel and rested her forehead against them.

Even with today's temperatures already climbing into the fifties, she felt chilled to the bone. Embarrassed and horrified, to boot.

The kernel of truth—her shaky financial situation—could make those rumors seem all the more credible.

She'd come here with little cash, and what she had, she'd been sinking into Thalia's property.

And with the growing population of animals at the shelter, she had a long, long list of equipment and supplies that she needed to buy.

But if one clerk in a tiny consignment shop had heard those rumors, how rampant were they? And how had they started? Her first thought had been Allan or his buddies, but that made no sense.

Surely even Allan could reason through the logic that he had *no* chance of trying to wheedle her out of money if she lost her job. And there'd be little return on the risk, if his old friends wanted to harass her. What would they gain?

These days a person with a credit card and Internet savvy could access legal records and frightening amounts of personal information for a bargain price…then twist the facts to do her harm. But why would anyone here be motivated to do that?

Yet there'd also been those footprints on the hill.

The anonymous note.

The night the dogs had gone wild out in the kennel.

She reached down and turned the heater to a higher setting as a chill crept deeper into her bones. If it was all related to the same perpetrator, then that person's actions were escalating, and she didn't want to find out what could happen next.

She lifted her gaze toward the sheriff's office down the street, then turned off the engine and climbed back out. It was time to pay the sheriff a visit.

TWELVE

"This was absolutely wonderful, Trace," Kris said, setting aside her fork. "Such an amazing meal."

The candlelight on the table centerpiece danced as a waitress passed by, sending the lean planes and angles of his face into sharp relief. "It's been a favorite of the locals for years. I think we all hope the tourists don't find out about it, because it's busy just as it is."

Quiet music filtered through the restaurant, and on a small dance floor in the far corner, an elderly couple followed the steps of a slow waltz in perfect harmony, as if they'd been dancing together all their lives.

"Isn't that sweet?" she murmured, canting her head in their direction. "The waitress said they celebrated their fiftieth anniversary last year. Do you like to dance?"

"It's out of my league. Would you like dessert? They have a white chocolate cheesecake here that Carrie orders every time."

At his swift change of topic, Kris caught her error. He'd once mentioned his rodeo days, and she'd seen him favor his leg more than once, especially on damp and chilly days. "What happened?"

He flashed a quick grin. "With the cheesecake? Carrie and I ordered it way too often, and we both gained fifty pounds. Easy."

"There couldn't be a spare ounce of fat on either of you anywhere," she teased.

"Looks can be so deceiving. Yours, for instance."

Her heart stumbled over all of the things in her past that he could mean, but then his eyes turned darker, smoky. And when his wicked grin kicked up a little higher, she felt a sense of reprieve.

"Oh?"

"Yes, ma'am. You wear jeans and baggy sweatshirts every day. And then you get all cleaned up and look like a rock star. Who knew?"

In her understated ivory outfit and simple gold chain she knew she was pretty much the polar opposite of a rock star, but his expression was so warm and intent that she felt her cheeks heat. "Tell me about yourself, cowboy."

He caught the eye of the waitress, then settled back in his chair. "Not much to say, really."

Kris felt the atmosphere cool a few degrees as he dropped his gaze to the multifaceted crystal ball between them that held a single votive.

"I don't mean personal stuff," she added with a laugh. "Just random. Like, Carrie tells me you've been a volunteer fireman *and* the county fire investigator for quite a while, yet I've never heard you mention either one. It all sounds fascinating."

"It's a way to give back." Mr. Conversationalist shifted his attention to a waitress who swooped in close. He spoke to her in a low tone and after she flitted away, he gave Kris an expectant look. "So tell me about you."

"That's fair, I guess. I think I mentioned that I grew up in various small towns around Battle Lake. Foster care, after my mom disappeared."

"Your dad?"

"Died when I was just a toddler. My sister, Emma, was in the system, too, but I haven't seen her in many years. Once I have enough money, I plan to start searching for her again."

The sudden warmth and compassion in his eyes was so strong, so mesmerizing, that for a moment she forgot to breathe.

"So you've been on your own for a long time."

She lifted a shoulder. "With the exception of a very youthful error in judgment when I met my ex-husband. Isn't there a saying, 'marry in haste, repent at leisure'? We were wrong for each other, and that pretty much ended my longing for family ties. Except for finding my sister Emma—but that search is on hold until I can hire another investigator."

"And that's why you came here, so determined to sell and move on?"

It was her turn to feel uncomfortable, but she forced

herself to meet his gaze squarely. "My ex-husband Allan and his friends got into serious trouble, and I ended up getting involved. With those legal costs plus his staggering amount of debt—in my name, as well— I've been struggling ever since. Fixing up Thalia's estate is taking every penny I've got, and the real estate taxes alone will probably wipe me out. I'll have no choice but to put it on the market."

"Carrie mentioned that you want to go back to school, too."

"I've thought about it for years, though I'm finding the animal shelter is really rewarding. So now, I'm not as sure." She gave a casual, dismissive wave of her hand. "That's me in a hundred words or less. I want to hear more about the firefighting part of *your* life. I think that sounds so amazing— and exciting."

He gave a low laugh. "In the movies. In real life it can be hot, exhausting and miserable. Long hours, often in the middle of the night. Sometimes it can be so tragic that it brings you to your knees."

"I don't think I could handle it."

"We actually do have four very capable women, and I'm glad to work beside them any day."

"But it sounds awfully hard for all of you." She thought she knew the answer, but she asked him anyway. "So what's the biggest reward?"

"This is a small community. People need to pull together. We save people's homes, businesses and their lives. Like I said, it's a way to give back."

His words were too pat, too practiced, to be complete. "And?"

The waitress returned with two slices of white chocolate cheesecake garnished with a dollop of dark chocolate whip cream and a cherry on the side, then she disappeared.

Trace took a bite of his, savored it, and set aside his fork. His mouth lifted into a brief, faint smile, as if he knew he might as well give in and tell her, even if it was hard to share. "I spent a few weeks every summer at my aunt and uncle's place as a kid. Uncle Jess was a wonderful guy, with twin boys my age." The shadows in his eyes deepened. "I went off with some buddies for the afternoon, hiking and swimming down at the creek—and then I heard fire engines. We all got excited, thinking something cool was happening in town, so we ran back, whooping and hollering. When I got there, my uncle had already died trying to save my cousins."

"Oh, Trace. I'm so sorry."

"No one ever figured out the cause of the fire. For the rest of her life my aunt was left to grieve, not knowing if she'd been partly to blame…and I felt the same way. What if I'd left something plugged in that sparked? And what if I'd stayed home and played with my cousins instead of going off on my own? Maybe I could've seen the flames and gotten everyone out."

"Or maybe you would've died, too. It must've been a fast fire to trap them like that."

"I want to think I could have made a difference."

"So now you do, as a firefighter."

He shrugged.

"And you do those fire investigations so other people won't be left without answers."

He looked at her from across the table. "That, and to deal with a bad case of survivor's guilt, I guess. Carrie keeps badgering me to do less, but I just…can't."

Kris already knew he was a responsible, hard-working and capable man, but the depth of emotion in his eyes touched her heart. "She's really proud of you, Trace. And I can see why."

"If she is, she's still totally naive. Because I'm not someone to be proud of at all."

They lingered for a while longer over their decadent desserts, then Trace drove her home. They kept up a light conversation all the way there…though Trace's surprising, final statement in the restaurant still sat between them like an elephant in the room.

She understood that he didn't want to elaborate, knew that the pain of it was far fresher than the fire of his youth. If he didn't want to share, so be it.

Back at Wind Hill she'd left a light on in the kitchen, but he still insisted on walking her to the door.

She shivered a little as she fumbled with her keys, thinking about good-night kisses and imagining the pleasure his touch might bring…but still knowing this relationship wasn't at that place and never would be.

From the corner of her eye she caught a dark, low

shadow bounding through the pool of light beneath the security lamp near the house. She spun around, nearly losing her balance on her three-inch heels. "Good heavens—what was *that?*"

"A coyote maybe?"

The shape froze for a moment, then turned for the house. As it drew closer, she saw it was one of the strays that had come in just yesterday.

"How on earth…" She stared as the dog came to the edge of the porch steps and woofed once, wagging its tail. "Before I left home, I checked every pen and I shut the exterior doors tight. Just like always. He *couldn't* have gotten free. Not on his own."

Trace glanced at her flimsy shoes. "Change your clothes quick. I'll take this dog and run down there to start checking on things."

"I'll be right out." She hurried inside, pulled on a pair of coveralls over her good clothes, yanked on a pair of boots, grabbed a coat and ran for the kennels, her heart pounding.

What if a grizzly had torn off a door and had attacked the helpless animals inside? What if—

Trace stepped out of the kennel, his face a grim mask. "Every one of the dogs is gone. The gates are all unlocked. Someone tossed the office, too, and made quite a mess."

Stunned, she pulled to a stop in front of him. "*All* of them?"

"All but the puppies. The cats and small pets are still there, too."

Alarm rushed through her over what had happened while she was out enjoying her dinner. "Blood—is there any blood? Were any of them hurt?"

"Nothing I could see."

"So…it wasn't a bear, then."

"Not unless a bear can manage those safety latches—which I doubt. A grizzly could tear them apart, but these were all unlocked."

She closed her eyes, thinking over the past week. "The dogs have been going crazy at night. It first happened Saturday after midnight. Ken came out to look, but he didn't see any wool or bear tracks—only people's footprints. So then I figured the dogs were maybe just barking at wolf calls from up in the hills."

"Do you have any idea who could've done this?"

"A few thoughts…but the thing right now is that I *have* to find those dogs. Six of them are on antibiotics, and the vet has bandaging on several. The scent of those wounds could make them very easy prey. And Lucy—poor Lucy will never make it on her own."

Trace looked up from his cell phone, his finger poised over the keypad. "Lucy?"

"An old fellow brought in his beloved old Brittany recently because he just couldn't care for her anymore. She's as feeble as he is, and she was a house pet all her life. She won't last a day out there."

Trace punched in a number, spoke to the dispatcher, then clipped the phone to his waist. "A couple of deputies are on their way. The dispatcher wants to know if you want her to run up some volunteers."

"In the dark? No…wait, yes—tell her yes. With enough people combing the woods nearby, maybe we can round a lot of the dogs up and get them back to safety. If even one of them dies…" She said a swift, silent prayer, then hurried into the office to paw through the rubble for the two flashlights she kept on the shelf.

When she came back outside, Trace was talking to someone on the phone. "I'm going," she mouthed, gesturing toward the woods. "I'll head east—"

He broke away from the call. "*No*—let me go with you. It's safer that way. We don't want to range too far at any rate—some volunteers are on their way, and you'll need to give them directions."

"But at least I—"

"I'm getting my rifle, and we're going together. The last thing we want to do is get separated or lost out there—especially since we don't know who might be waiting."

THIRTEEN

Sam Martin and a half-dozen sleepy-looking adults showed up within the hour, flashlights in hand. They stood by the kennel and whispered amongst themselves until Kris caught their attention.

"Trace and I have found five dogs so far. They hadn't gone far, and they responded to our calls. That leaves twenty-eight of them on the loose. If they took off running we won't have a chance tonight…but I'm guessing that most are close by. Some might even come back, knowing they have food and shelter here.

"I understand that Sam gave you all whistles—give a long whistle if you find a dog. Two blasts if you found one and need help. That way we can all keep a running tally of what we have left. Grab some leashes, and fan out. Can we meet back here in an hour?"

The volunteers—mostly middle-aged women—nodded in agreement, then headed across the clearing.

"You should stay here, Trace," Kris said. "You can coordinate the efforts and make sure everyone is accounted for in case some of these gals head for home early."

"I'm going with you."

"You're limping. It's hard going out there in the dark."

"That's nothing new," he growled. "Let's go. No one headed straight north, and we haven't been up there, either."

"But—"

"You can stay here. I'm not. And I'm not limping."

She threw up her hands in frustration and joined him in a few strides. "Whatever you say, cowboy. Just remember that I probably can't carry you back."

At the top of the hill overlooking the ranch, she stopped and looked back. "You saw footprints up here, once. Do you suppose it was the same person who let the dogs loose?"

"Maybe."

She slipped on an icy patch and had to grab for some branches to keep from going down. Trace shot an amused look at her but kept walking. "Are you sure you're okay? Maybe *you* should head back."

"No." Despite the chilly night air, the return of his dry humor warmed her clear to her toes. "But I—"

From somewhere to the south came a single, long whistle. Farther east, another.

"Two found—that makes twenty-six to go," she said. "I'm praying for every one of them to show up tonight."

He stopped at the top of another rise and started calling for the dogs. She joined in, then they stood rock still and listened. *Nothing.*

"Maybe they all just formed a pack and took the easy route—downhill to the east," she muttered, straining to hear. She swung the flashlight in a wide arc, illuminating bare tree branches, scrub brush and snow-covered boulders.

Trace started down an incline. "You never know. Let's go farther."

Halfway down he slipped and went down hard against a fallen tree. When she reached him, his mouth was a grim line. "Are you okay?"

He struggled back to his feet, favoring his left leg. "I'm good. Let's go."

A long, single whistle sounded from beyond them, then another. Her heart lifted. "Twenty-four left. I'm so grateful that those people were willing to come."

Trace soldiered on, his uneven gait more pronounced. "I thought I saw fresh dog tracks back aways. I want to cover at least another mile before we head for home tonight, just in case I'm right. Can you make it that far?"

Sheltered from the daytime sun, the snow was deeper here, hiding low-lying stumps and rocks, and making the going difficult. Winded, she paused. "No problem. I plan to go all night, if I have to."

From somewhere far ahead came the keening of the wind rushing through a stand of pines...or was it? "Wait—did you hear that?"

Trace stopped to listen.

Again, it came, faint and high. But it wasn't the wind. It was a dog, though whether it was crying in pain or terror she couldn't tell. "Over there—more to the north."

"Got it. Maybe a half mile or so ahead."

He adjusted his direction and continued at a steady pace, though now and then she saw him grab on to a tree trunk and take a long, steadying breath.

"I can go on ahead," she called out. "You could wait here, and if it's one of the dogs, I can bring it back on my own."

"No." He stopped and waited for her to catch up. "You don't know what's out here. And we're not going to split up. We go together, or not at all."

She hesitated. "I want to get to that dog. But if this terrain is going to tear up your knee, then it isn't worth it. What happened to you, anyway?"

He didn't answer, just started on again, skirted a heavy stand of brush and began climbing the next steep slope.

Stubborn man. "Just remember that I thought you should stop," she muttered, "when you're in traction and a cast."

He glanced back with an amused expression. "I heard that, and it isn't going to happen."

They were moving deeper and deeper into dense, unfamiliar timber, where rocky shelves rose high on one side and boulders littered the ground.

"Hear that?" He stopped. "More to the left, I think."

After another fifty yards she heard it, too; the weak cry of an animal in pain, then a long silence. Whatever it was, it seemed to be losing ground.

Trace adjusted their direction and they both walked in silence, listening.

He suddenly skidded to a halt, and braced a hand

against a tree in front of him for support, then swung his flashlight in a slow arc. "This isn't good. Kris."

She slowly made her way to his side and stared over the edge of what appeared to be a large, deep pit maybe forty feet square, and a good twenty to thirty feet deep. The loose shale walls were steep and boulders littered the floor.

Trace pointed the flashlight to a rocky ledge maybe ten feet from the bottom. "See?"

"Oh, *no.*" Kris held a hand at her mouth as she stared down at Lucy. The dog was stretched on her side, and blood matted the silky feathers of one of her front legs. Even at this distance she could see the animal was breathing hard. "She couldn't have found a worse place in the whole area."

"I'll bet she was trying to go back home."

The image of the old dog desperately trying to find her master made Kris's eyes burn. She blinked and focused on the walls of the dog's prison. "We can't leave her there. She'll die. What about over on the other side—it's not quite as steep."

"I'll have to go down right above her. How many leashes you have?"

"Wait—you can't do that. Your leg—"

"It has to be me. Are you strong enough to climb back up with her?"

"But—"

"And you have to stay up here so you can take her from me. It's the only way, unless you plan to come back tomorrow with more equipment and people."

"We can't wait. I just don't want you to get hurt, either."

"Loop your leashes together. They're nylon, so they ought to hold well enough for a safety rope in case I slip. Do we have enough? I think it's about a twenty-foot drop there, and we still need a good, solid wrap around a tree at the top."

"I've got about fifteen feet of nylon cord in my pocket, too. Maybe you can use it for a sling over your shoulder, so you can support her better on the way up." She fashioned a rope out of the five leashes, then jerked off her boots and took off her knee-high socks while Trace took off his heavy coat. "Here—you can used these for her leg if you have to."

The temperature had warmed today, turning the snow to slush. But now it was steadily dropping. She could feel the extra bite in the air, and patchy ice was forming where the snow had melted. She peered over the edge once again at the narrow rocky outcroppings of shale. Some were glittering with treacherous ice. Many looked thin and fragile.

Trace shoved the extra nylon cord in his pocket, snapped his flashlight to one of his belt loops, then fastened the makeshift rope around his narrow waist. He tied the other end around a tree close to the edge.

He tossed his phone to her. "If things go badly, move around a little until you can get reception, then call for help. We're about a mile due south of my place, just below Blackfoot Ridge."

"Please—be careful." She helped steady him as he

started slowly down the vertical surface, holding the flashlight with one hand and letting the rope slowly feed through the other. And then she started to pray.

God…we're trying to save one of Your dear creatures, and the heart of an elderly man. It will hurt him so if anything happens to his old friend. Please, please guide Trace's footsteps and keep him safe…and give him the strength to make it back up. Please…

The rope jerked. Pebbles bounced and clattered down the cliff. Dropping the flashlight, she grabbed the line with both hands, bracing her feet against a rock and trying to hold it steady while Trace fought to regain his footing.

"I'm…I'm okay," he called out. "Almost there."

A minute later, the line went slack, and panic rushed through her. *"Trace!"*

"I'm good—I'm at the bottom."

Holding on to the trunk of a slender tree, she leaned over the edge and saw him sweep his flashlight beam over the dog. He bent over her wounded leg for several long minutes before straightening and in the dim wash of moonlight, she could see him surveying the steep surrounding walls.

"There's no other good way out, I guess, but this is going to be slow. I'll need you to light the way, if you can."

He bent over the dog again and fashioned a crude net with the extra nylon rope, then gently picked her up and took the first step up. Lucy whimpered and struggled in his arms and he slipped back down.

"We've got to do this differently," he muttered. He bent over her again, retying the rope into a more secure carrier, then tying it to the safety line he'd used on the way down.

"I've got to be down here to guide and lift her, but I need you to help some by pulling on the line as she comes up…can you handle that? Otherwise we'll never make it—I need at least one hand for the climb."

"Got it." Kris pulled the line up, hand over hand, by painstaking inches. Twice, Trace slipped backward, though Lucy—clearly terrified into frozen silence—stayed secure.

When both the dog and Trace finally reached the top, Lucy staggered a few feet and then flopped to her side, exhausted by her ordeal.

"I don't know who to hug—you or the dog," Kris exclaimed with joyous relief. "This was the longest half hour of my life."

She leaned over the dog and stroked her head, then inspected the foreleg matted with blood. "I was afraid her leg was broken, but it doesn't look like it. She did bear weight on all fours for a few strides."

"I agree. She's not up to walking all the way back, though."

"Then we can take turns carrying her. She isn't that heavy—I weighed her when she arrived, and she was just a shade under thirty pounds. And it really isn't that far back."

He looked up from the leashes he was untying and laughed. "I think you must've developed amnesia from all the excitement, but if you're game, that's fine with me. Let me start carrying her, though."

He snapped one leash on Lucy's collar, handed Kris the others, then he gathered the dog in his arms and started making his way through the snow.

The sight of him—a big, broad-shouldered man so gently cradling an old dog, moving so carefully to avoid jostling her, did something warm and wonderful to Kris's jaded heart. She could imagine him with an armload of toddlers at bedtime, a big bear of a man who nurtured the most tender little heart, who kept those children safe and who guarded their futures with exquisite care.

What would it be like to love a man like him? To be with him forever, until they both grew old? She would probably never know.

He would be a wonderful father someday, but he would never be a part of her life. His roots went deep here. She would have to leave.

But for as long as she lived, she knew she would never forget the image of Trace Randall helping her save the life of an old man's beloved friend.

FOURTEEN

Trace forced himself to step down from his pickup and walk toward the Wind Hill kennel with an even stride the next morning, even though searing pain shot through his knee with every step.

He'd managed to pull off yesterday's late-night search without stirring up Kris's worries, and he wasn't going to let his guard drop today, either.

One woman hovering was enough…and Carrie had enough energy for three.

"Kris?" he called out as he opened the office door.

The place had been pristine until last night, but now it was in shambles, papers and supplies thrown everywhere, the stainless-steel exam table turned on its side. It was a display of senseless violence that made his adrenaline surge—and it had been directed against someone who wouldn't stand a chance if this guy came after her.

What kind of sick jerk would do this—and why? It spoke of rage and power and of wanting to leave a message. *A threat.*

Trace could think of a message or two he'd like to give the perpetrator, but neither of them were legal. Even a well-deserved uppercut to the guy's jaw could mean landing in jail himself.

And a person like this wasn't worth it.

He took a steadying breath to calm his anger as he went into the kennel area of the building. "Kris? Are you here?"

Half of the runs were still empty, their front gates ajar. The remaining dogs barked and whined and scrambled against the chain-link barrier for attention.

Lucy was curled up with Bailey in a big cardboard box filled with soft blankets at the end of the aisle, clearly receiving special dispensation after her adventure.

"Where's Kris, old girl—do you know?"

Both dogs raised their heads to acknowledge the interruption, then blissfully sank back into their warm nest.

"If they know, they're not telling."

Trace turned around to find Carrie standing in the aisle, her hands on her hips. "What are you doing here?"

She winked at him. "I could ask you the same thing."

"I came again to see if I could help. Looks like a lot of animals are still missing."

She nodded. "I've been out searching with the volunteers since seven this morning. Someone picked up several of the dogs wandering down the highway, where they could've been killed. A couple of others were found several miles away in someone's yard. A deputy is bringing those dogs in shortly, or so I heard."

"I'd sure like to find the person who turned them loose."

She shook her head, "Unfortunately, a lot of the volunteers are saying that Kris is just careless and lazy because this kind of thing never happened at the old facility. They're thinking the trashed office was a way for her to cover it up so it would *look* like an intruder had been here."

"That's crazy."

"It gets worse. Apparently rumors are flying about Kris and her ex dealing drugs and even doing time. One of the women said a store clerk in town refused to take a check from her last week, because she 'knew' Kris was in deep financial trouble and figured it would bounce. The clerk claimed that when she said she would only take cash, Kris threatened her."

"At this rate, it will be a miracle if she doesn't just decide to sell out now and move out of town."

"That's what I think. I mean, where is all of this coming from? She's been here almost two months and suddenly it's like a smear campaign. If a popularity poll was taken right now, her name would be in the gutter." Carrie glanced at all the empty pens. "And you can bet that if some of these dogs get hit or disappear for good, this town will never forgive her."

Yet Trace had seen her horror last night when she'd discovered the missing dogs. He'd witnessed her absolute determination to go after every single one of them, and only a long argument had convinced her to give up her search at three in the morning.

Even on the long hike back with Lucy, she'd insisted on carrying the dog most of the way.

If that was the behavior of a woman with callous disregard for the animals in her care, he'd eat his best boots.

She'd once said that she'd had a troubled past, but a lot of people did foolish things when they were young, learned from their mistakes, then went on to live honorable lives.

If she was still guilty as charged by the good folks of Battle Creek regarding those other issues, he'd eat his spurs right along with 'em.

"So where is Kris now?" he asked, starting for the door.

Carrie's eyes widened. "You're *hurt,* Trace. You need to prop that leg up with ice packs and rest, not go gallivanting all over the county. I'm going to call that doctor again and get you an appointment."

"I'm just fine, and he's going to get real tired of me canceling. Pretty soon he isn't even going to *take* your calls."

She strode right up to him, grabbed his forearms and glared up into his face. "You know what that surgeon said."

He tried to gently extricate himself from her grip, then gave up. "I can't just sit around and baby an old injury, or my ranch could fail. And if I don't help my neighbors when they need it, maybe they will."

"If you last that long. Goals can change, Trace. Circumstances do. Things can be out of our control."

"The good Lord willing, this ranch could be financially secure in another five years, cattle prices stabilize, and we get enough rain."

"It's a wonderful goal, it truly is, but maybe you need to form a partnership with someone. But I'm only telling you what the surgeon told me—push yourself too hard, and you'll blow that knee. And there's only so many times it can be repaired."

During the next few days, cars pulled in now and then with another one of the refugees. Only eight dogs were still loose by the following weekend, but where they were was anyone's guess.

It didn't take guesswork to know about the gossip spreading through the area, though. Kris had overheard the volunteer search party talking between themselves. People at the drugstore a few aisles over, who hadn't realized she was there. Even after church on Sunday, out in the parking lot.

Trying to fight it all with the truth would be like trying to stop a leak in the Hoover Dam with bubblegum.

Trace and Carrie hadn't been over since and she hadn't even seen them in church, so she was pretty sure they'd been hearing the rumors, too...and were probably taking care to establish careful distance from the mess her life had become. That was the part that hurt the most, though had she ever really thought there was a chance with Trace?

She was drawn to him on every level. His strength,

his determination. His quiet, easy wit. The fact that it made her heart warm just hearing his voice. If she'd ever allowed herself to dream, he was the kind of guy she would've imagined.

But there was no way she could stay at Wind Hill forever. She needed the sale money for clearing her debts and to resume her search for Emma. She did need to leave, while his roots were here.

So maybe it was a blessing to have a clean break now…before her foolish feelings for him grew too deep.

Now, she stood in the kennel office as an installation tech finished putting in the security system and wondered if the expense had even been worth it.

The county board met on the second Tuesday evening of the month, and she could only imagine the heated discussion they were having right now—one that might culminate in a formal letter rescinding her provisional contract as the county's animal shelter. Would she need to put the place up for sale far sooner than she'd thought?

"This security system will operate just like the one you installed up at the house, right?"

"Yes, ma'am. If a smoke detector is triggered, it sounds a loud alarm here and alerts our call center. That operator calls your local 911 system. You can also trigger it by touching a button on the control panel. Same thing if someone forces open a door or window. You have five minutes to call the service number and cancel."

"And you haven't seen any problems with it?"

He shrugged. "Every company is different, and even this one offers a tier of features and service. You have the most basic level, but it'll get the job done…unless your phone service is interrupted."

"But the on-site alarms would still go off."

"Definitely…and they do have battery backups that should last at least twelve hours if the power goes off. When I get done here, I'll overnight your signed contract to our main office. You should be good to go by sometime tomorrow."

"Good enough, then."

"Yep—so the next time the dogs all go for a walk, you'll know," he added with deep laugh.

She could barely summon a smile in response. "There isn't going to *be* a next time if I can help it. Tell your boss thanks for fitting this in after hours."

"Will do." He held out a clipboard. "Just sign the form and I'll be going. On my way home, I'll put some security system signs on your outbuildings. That should warn off anyone thinking this will be an easy place to hit."

She signed the paper and handed it back, then watched him gather his tools and walk out to his truck. Even this guy had apparently heard about the incident, and *he'd* come from clear over in Copper Cliff.

With a sigh, she grabbed her keys from the desk drawer, locked the place behind her and headed out into the dark to her SUV. After a quick run into town to load up on supplies for the week, she'd come back to heat up something easy for supper, then settle down with a good book.

Or perhaps she'd better start searching the Internet.

She'd hoped to stay a year, to work on sprucing the place up for a far better sale price. Maybe, somewhere deep in her heart, she'd even hoped she could find a way to stay forever.

But settling for a quick sale and looking at the job market somewhere else might end up being her only option…even if it meant leaving Trace—and a part of her heart—behind.

There was a definite warm, teasing hint of spring in the air when she let Bailey outside the next morning. The night had stayed well above freezing, and now pools of water stood like mirrors out in the meadow where there'd once been massive drifts of snow.

The clerk in the grocery store last night had warned about snowfalls that could come even in late May, and from her childhood experiences, Kris knew it was true. But for now, the scents of damp earth and pine and a gentle breeze from the south filled her with joy. *Thank You, Lord, for this beautiful day…for the chance to be here in this glorious place, if only for a while.*

Bailey headed straight for the nearest pool of water and splashed into the center, then rolled ecstatically.

"Bailey!"

The old dog lifted his head in her direction, then romped through the water like an arthritic pup before shaking himself off and trotting back to the house.

Her cell phone rang, and the light moment faded when she read the caller ID on the screen.

"Sheriff Carpenter?"

He cleared his throat. "I thought you should know about the board meeting last night."

She froze, unable to speak. Last night she'd had a hard time falling asleep, until she'd started praying and finally made herself give the whole situation over to God.

But now, the sheriff's words made her feel as if she'd been hit with a bucket of ice water.

"We're aware of the rumors in town. So, before the meeting, the board supervisor asked me to do a little checking."

She swallowed hard. "And?"

"I know your ex-husband was involved in illegal activities. I'm looking at his record right now. I also see you were charged only with possession, got probation, and that you testified for the prosecution during his trial. Is that correct?"

The weight of her past settled heavily on her shoulders; a mantle of guilt and regret worse than any sentence or probation because she knew it would never, ever go away. "That part of my life is long over. I promise you that I'm telling the truth."

"I talked to your probation officer earlier today."

Kris held her breath, remembering the steely-eyed, silver-haired gentleman she'd had to meet for three long years. Oddly enough, the man had become more of a father figure to her than anyone else in her life…though she knew she was just one of the count-less others in his daily routine. Would he even remember how hard she'd tried to turn her life around?

"And?"

"He says you had a tough life. That you fell in with the wrong crowd, but that of all the people he's ever worked with, you were one with the greatest poten-tial. He sounded really proud of you."

A feeling of warmth spread through her. "He's a good man. His advice helped me more than I can say."

She heard the sound of rustling papers.

"I also checked your legal records since then. No trouble, not so much as a parking ticket. And your credit score is excellent, so you obviously pay your debts on time, without fail. In other words, the rumors around here are wrong. I don't think it's the usual gossip, my dear, though that is bad enough. Someone wants to cause you trouble."

"I know."

"We barely have enough manpower to address our most serious issues, so I can't delve into this as much as I want to. But I'm concerned about the escalating pattern. Particularly, the night the dogs got loose."

"As I told Sam, each of the individual dog pens was closed. There's no way all of the latches could've 'in-advertently' opened on their own. And there's no way I could've left every last one of them open, either—no way at all. I would've had over two dozen dogs fol-lowing me straight out of the building."

"Makes sense."

"What about fingerprints?"

"None of 'em matched anything in the AFIS system. They were all the same—yours. So if anyone else was there, they likely were smart enough to use gloves."

"And there are no other suspects?"

"We checked out some of the people who'd wanted the county animal shelter contract, but they vehemently denied causing any trouble. One even begged for a lie detector test to prove he didn't do it. Said he'd pay the full cost to have it done, just to prove his innocence."

"So who could be behind it all? There's been no word from my ex-husband lately, and I've never heard from his buddies. I know that the Bascombs left the area. Have you had trouble with vandals here? Teenagers, looking for a little excitement?"

"It's always possible. We'll check on any news about your husband's friends and see if they've ever surfaced. I know the authorities want them back, so they might be in custody by now. I can also send Sam out to recheck the Bascomb place, and since he's on the night shift in your area, I'll remind him to cruise by your place now and then. Other than that, I'm afraid we'll just have to wait and see."

"Have you been missing me, sweetheart?"

At the sound of Allan's voice, Kris jerked to a halt. Just this morning she'd told the sheriff that she hadn't heard from him in a long while. His was the last voice she wanted to hear.

"Got nothing to say?" He chuckled, his self-satis-faction clear. "Maybe a little face-to-face time would help. Say, in an hour or two?"

"Y-you're here? In Montana?"

"Why not? Takin' a little vacation, checking the place out. You really got lucky, babe. Nice view."

Her thoughts rocketed to the night the dogs had gotten loose. "You've been here."

"You weren't around, but oh, well. I had a nice tour anyway. My buddies and I couldn't stick around till you got back, though."

Anger bubbled up into her throat, fierce and hot. "Were you in the kennels?"

He made a sound of disgust. "Not my thing. Why are you doing that anyway? You could sell that place and make a fortune."

She bit back a sharp reply. He didn't deserve an ex-planation, but if he was in the area, she didn't want to antagonize him, either. "I…don't think so."

"Whatever. I'm just giving you some good advice."

She didn't respond.

He laughed. "You sound worried, babe. But you don't need to be. We were just passing through."

With two guys who had violated their parole, it didn't sound like a little vacation. "Have fun."

"We all had a talk. Decided that we're going to let the past go, if you know what I mean."

After seeing Thalia's property? The unlikelihood of *that* change of heart almost made Kris laugh. "I'm glad."

"I mean it." Allan's voice softened. "We had good times, you and me. A lot of them. Maybe sometime we can give each other another chance. I've never found anyone else like you. Ever."

At eighteen, she'd fallen for his chameleon-like ability to charm her when she least expected it. She wasn't falling for it now. "Have a good trip, Allan." She paused, as if looking at the time. "Sorry—I've got to go."

"So do I. But I promise, I'll be seeing you again soon. Real, real soon."

FIFTEEN

With most of the dogs back in the kennels and other animals coming and going as part of the shelter business, Kris stayed busy. Though she kept a sharp eye out for any sign of Allan, he didn't show up…and now she'd begun to think that his call had been a ruse, that he might have called on his cell phone from Idaho just to unsettle her.

The one empty spot in her life was Trace, who hadn't been over since the day after the dogs escaped. She could understand why—anyone hearing about her checkered past would surely want to keep their distance.

But even Carrie hadn't called until the day after the security system was installed, and she'd sounded oddly distant. Her vague promise to stop by soon was clearly just an easy way to end an awkward conversation.

So when she did stop by on Friday morning with a dozen of her grandmother's wonderful caramel rolls and an offer of a girls' night out at the little movie theater in Battle Creek, Kris stared at her for a moment, unsure.

"I didn't think I'd hear from either of you again," she finally managed. "With all that has happened, I'd understand."

"We've been really busy." Without quite meeting Kris's eyes, Carrie flapped a hand dismissively, then rested her elbow in the open window of her truck. "I've been meaning to get back over here for ages, though."

Kris bit her lower lip, not wanting to ask, yet not able to hold back the words, either. "And Trace…. how's he doing?"

Carrie hesitated for just a split second. "Good, good. It's been a *really* busy week for both of us, but he'll stop by one of these days. The movie starts at seven, and we could get a pizza after. So do you want me to come pick you up tonight?"

From the swift change of subject, Kris knew he wouldn't be stopping by anytime soon. But then, what else had she expected? "You're on the way to town for me. Let me drive."

"You got it. See you in a few hours."

After taking care of all the late afternoon chores down at the kennel, Kris left Bailey in his comfy dog bed with the run of the place, locked the doors and turned on the security system, then hurried up to the house to get showered and changed.

In less than an hour, she drove past the main house at the Rocking R, and turned down the lane to Carrie's cabin.

Though she'd promised herself that she wouldn't even look, she glanced around as she passed the house and barns. There was no sign of Trace anywhere.

"Perfect timing," Carrie exclaimed as she came out the door and climbed into the SUV. "This should be fun. I never miss a DiCaprio movie. Most of them I see twice in the theater, and then I buy the DVD. I haven't seen this one even once, yet."

"A red-letter night, then," Kris teased.

"You bet. And it's been a long, long time since I've been out on the town, too. My social life is beyond boring. Not that I'm looking, though. It'll be a while before the thought of dating even sounds halfway appealing—if ever."

Kris shot a sideways glance at her across the front seat as she turned the SUV toward the highway. With Carrie's gleaming dark hair and sparkling brown eyes, she looked like an effervescent model for a shampoo commercial. "I have a feeling that the local guys are going to sit up and take notice way before that."

"Like I'd be interested. That's one road I don't want to travel again." Carrie rolled her eyes. "I'm done with men for *good*. At least Billy stays away now that I'm at Trace's place. You, on the other hand, have been single a long time. I'm surprised you haven't hooked up with some cool guy by now."

"Various complications and bad memories can be a

powerful antidote to all that," Kris said with a light laugh. "We're quite a trio, aren't we? You, Trace and me."

"When I start thinking too hard about my life, I try to step back and accept that where I am is where I was meant to be. Teaching at Battle Creek. Being there for my brother. Helping with Sunday school at the church. Maybe someday I'll be led to something different in life, but right now, I'm content. How about you?"

Other than the local gossips, Allan lurking around, and someone who wants to see my business fail, I'm just dandy. But in a few months, it would all be behind her, and talking about it would just put a damper on the whole evening.

"I'm good. Let's make a promise, though—no matter where we end up, we'll keep in touch at least once a year."

Carrie twisted in her seat. "So you *are* thinking about leaving, then."

"No firm decisions. I'd like to stay, truly…but on the other hand, maybe my ideas about fixing up Wind Hill weren't the best because so much depends on the real estate market and interest rates. I'll just have to see. But whatever happens, I'd still like to stay in touch with you."

The movie was wonderful as Carrie had predicted. The pizza was loaded with cheese and was one of the best Kris had ever eaten. But after their conversation on the way to town, Carrie stayed subdued and thoughtful.

When Kris dropped her off at the Rocking R at midnight, Carrie opened the door and unbuckled her seat belt, then hesitated at the door of the SUV. "If there's anything I can do to help you, say the word, okay? I mean, I know things haven't been easy here. We'd really like you to stay in Montana."

We? Kris doubted that, but she still dredged up a smile. "Thanks."

"Well…you take care, hear? Maybe we can meet for lunch next Saturday or something."

"That sounds great." Kris waved, then did a U-turn and started for the highway, drumming her fingernails on the steering wheel as the miles slipped past. She slowed and turned off the highway onto the lane leading to Wind Hill Ranch.

It *had* been an enjoyable night. Mostly.

Carrie had seemed uncomfortable, but maybe that was because she'd felt the stares of some of the locals in the pizza place, and at the theater. In a town this small, not a lot happened, so any local excitement was great fodder for conversation.

Kris was probably red-letter, balloons-and-confetti material for the gossips.

That first time Kris had attended church the news had even made the "Out and About" column in the tiny local newspaper, along with a breathless announcement about the Anderson family's visitors from Billings.

The memory made her smile. The local lady gathering tidbits for the column probably didn't realize it, but maybe Kris's visit *did* deserve mention. That Sunday had made a difference in her life already, and even now she felt an ember of warmth in her heart that hadn't been there for years.

The acrid odor of smoke started coming in through the front vents on the dashboard. She dropped her gaze to the heat gauge. *Normal.* She slowed and scanned the timber surrounding the lane. It was all darkness out here, save for the arc of her headlights....

And then, around the next curve, she could see slivers of crimson pulsing between the dense stand of pines ahead.

Another hundred feet and she drew in a sharp, ragged breath of horror. Flames had engulfed the cabin and were shooting fifty to a hundred feet into the sky in a blinding, vicious inferno.

She accelerated in panic—then slammed on the brakes. There was nothing she could do. *Nothing.* Where were the fire trucks? The squad cars? Had they even received the alarm?

With numb, shaking fingers she punched 911 into her cell phone. After the call she opened the door of her SUV and felt a blast of heat slam against her face, even though she was still a good two hundred feet away.

A moment of rising panic grabbed her heart and she spun around. The kennel and barn were eerily illuminated by the wild, twisting flames. Both were intact, though—and Bailey was safe in the kennel. *Thank You, God.*

Her panic dissolved into sorrow as she turned to stare at the engulfed cabin. None of her own possessions mattered. She had no family mementos of her own. But everything of Thalia's had been brought back up to the cabin, and it was all gone. Artwork. Books. Every last vestige of a fascinating and unique woman…and with Emma gone and perhaps even dead, too, by now, every last family tie Kris had was in flames.

Something in the house exploded, sending a burst of embers skyward over the meadow, then it happened again and again. Each minute stretched into infinity as she waited, waited, waited for the sounds of approaching sirens.

Something hot burned across her cheek.

She stumbled back to the SUV and threw it into Reverse, then floored the accelerator. The tires spun wildly, then took hold and the vehicle shot across the meadow to the kennels. She rammed it into Park and stepped outside again.

Here, over the roar of the fire, she could hear the frantic barking of the dogs. But they were safe inside. Far enough away.

The mesmerizing, terrible fire was like a living creature reaching for the stars…the empty windows of the cabin glowing like a vision of hell.

At the far, shadowy edge of the meadow, she saw an abrupt movement. A glowing figure illuminated by the flames, too far away to make out. A man? And what was he holding?

He shifted and the long barrel of a rifle gleamed in the intense light of the fire.

Sirens. But the discordant wailing was too, too far away.

Please, God....please...

In heart-stopping slow motion she saw the figure turn toward her.

Now she could almost make out a face twisted with anger—or hatred—though the dark shadows and surging flames playing across his face rendered his features into something evil. Barely human.

He lifted the rifle high. Took aim.

She spun around, racing for the back of the SUV. Her foot caught on a muddy rut and she started to fall...

Something hot, searing, exploded at her ear.

And then everything went black.

SIXTEEN

Sirens wailed like banshees screaming inside her head. Lights spun in a dizzying whirl; red, blue, blinding white. Voices filled the air—a legion of people started running. Shouting orders.

She felt cold…so cold.

Blinking, she shifted her weight and felt icy water and mud squelch up between her fingers. She realized she was on the ground, her jeans and jacket soaked through.

She shivered as she struggled to sit up, the world still off-kilter, her head throbbing with some deafening jungle beat that threatened to drown out the melee.

The fire.

She blinked and fell back against the rear tire of the SUV in near darkness, stunned by the surging activity around the cabin—now just a blackened stone fireplace surrounded by charred, skeletal fingers clawing toward the sky and a jumble of burning logs.

A back wall collapsed with a rush of sparks and flames that spurted skyward, hungry, eager.

Lights bright as a circus filled the meadow. Spotlights. The headlights of rescue vehicles. Fire trucks. Patrol cars, their light bars still spinning. Beyond that, she could make out the gleaming bumpers of a cluster of cars—probably the volunteer firemen. Trace—was he here?

A wave of nausea pitched through her stomach, warring with…what was it? Pizza…she'd had pizza earlier, back when the world was normal and sane. Back when she'd had a cabin and Thalia's precious things in boxes…

Someone on the periphery of the action noticed her and called out. Suddenly, yellow slickered bodies crowded around her, their speech nonsensical and loud.

One of them leaned down and loomed into her face. He lifted off his helmet, and she realized he worked at the drugstore.

She floated into some misty, weightless place….

A hand touched her shoulder and an image of a firelit creature filled her thoughts. She fought against it, trying to escape. *A gun—did he have a gun?*

"Sit—don't move."

She instantly stilled, then shook her head to clear her scrambled thoughts. She looked up into the concerned expression of a different man looming over her. "Sh-sheriff?"

Someone else dropped to her side and tightened a blood pressure cuff around her arm, then flicked a flashlight on and off, in front of her eyes.

"Are you okay?"

"I—I think so." She reached for her cheek, expecting to find blood, but her hand came away with mud. She moved her hand higher and found a tender lump forming on her forehead.

"Can you stand up?"

When she nodded, he hooked an arm under hers and hoisted her to her feet.

"Can you make it over there?" he tipped his head at the open doors of an emergency rescue vehicle parked a few yards away. "They'll come get you if you can't"

"I...can." She tottered a few steps, then walked slowly with him at her side until he helped her sit on the bumper.

A matching vehicle was parked next to it, where an emergency crew with large, glowing EMT letters on the back of their slickers was working feverishly over a prone figure on a gurney.

One of them barked a command, then they worked as one to hoist it into the rear of the vehicle. In a few moments the vehicle was gone, lights flashing and its siren wailing into the night.

"W-what happened? Who was that?"

"You didn't see anyone else here?"

"I—I don't know." The pounding in her head intensified, making it harder to form the words. "I thought I saw something—someone. I think he shot at me, but I was falling...that's all I remember."

"Tell me what happened here tonight. Exactly what happened."

His voice was calm, but it held a thread of steel and she suddenly knew something was very, very wrong. And though she was already shaking from the cold, wet clothes that clung to her skin, now her blood turned to ice.

Someone draped a blanket over her shoulders and she gratefully grabbed at the edges, drawing it tighter.

"Kris?" he prodded. "We need to know."

"I—I went to town tonight—with Carrie Randall. We went for a movie and pizza. I dropped her at home and came here. Only…" She swallowed hard, then forced herself to go on. "Only the cabin was engulfed in flames. I don't understand. My new security system—why didn't it trigger an emergency call?" She searched the faces of the sheriff and the EMTs who now stood around her. "It should have. I lost *everything.* Everything of Thalia's…"

"But you saw no one except for someone in the distance who shot at you."

"Right."

The sheriff turned away and spoke to someone behind him in a low tone, then met her eyes once more. "You do have quite a knot on your head, so the EMTs want to get you checked out at the hospital. We'll probably have more questions for you tomorrow. You'll stay in town. Right?"

"No. I have to be here. The animals…"

"Were any in your cabin?" he asked gently. "We might find them running loose if they escaped…"

She closed her eyes briefly as relief washed through

her. "No. I left my dog out in the kennel for the night, since I was going to be out late."

"Your personal house pet?" The sheriff exchanged glances with another officer. "Is…that something you would often do when away?"

"Yes…no…" She faltered to a stop. "He sometimes has trouble with separation anxiety since I'm almost never away. He likes his bed in the kennel office, though, and I figured he'd be near the other dogs. Why?"

"Just curious. Lucky that he wasn't in the cabin."

Again, she caught the glances between the two men…and suddenly knew that they suspected her of arson. How could she ever prove that she hadn't lit the match?

But worse, someone had been injured. "Tell me— who did they take away in the ambulance?"

"Deputy Sam Martin. We found him in the weeds on the back side of the house, unconscious. He'd been shot, Kris…and right now, it doesn't look good for him."

The Battle Creek hospital was a small one—around twenty long-term beds, plus a half dozen earmarked for the emergency room. With just a bare-bones staff on the best of days, it was even lighter at night.

By the time a radiologist and a physician finished with Sam and a helicopter had airlifted him to Billings, it was nearly two in the morning.

By the time Kris's own X-rays, labs and a CT scan

were complete and evaluated—all fine—dawn was breaking over the eastern horizon, and she was exhausted.

And now, she was in town without a vehicle.

She started to dial Carrie's number but then ended the call, knowing that her friend had gotten to bed late and was probably still sleeping.

And calling Trace? No way.

At eight, Kris paged through the slim telephone book in the waiting room and dialed the home number for Polly Norcross. It took just a minute of explanation before Polly interrupted her with a brisk promise to be at the hospital in ten minutes.

Kris went outside to sit on one of the benches and wait.

Good as her word, Polly soon pulled up at the E.R. doors in an ancient silver Horizon and waved. "I'm an early riser," she chirped. "Glad to help out—but I am *horrified* to think about all you've been through. And that poor deputy. Oh, my!"

On the drive out to Wind Hill, Kris told her the whole story. When Polly pulled to a stop in front of the damp smoldering remains of the cabin, her mouth sagged open in horror.

"Land sakes," she muttered after a long pause. "This is just hard to believe. How many times was I here, visiting your dear aunt? And now it's gone. All gone."

They both got out of Polly's car and moved closer, circling the acrid cinders and charred beams. Here, twisted water pipes hung in arcs at a crazy angle. There, the blackened remnants of appliances and plumbing fixtures had been haphazardly tossed.

"I was hoping I'd be able to salvage some of Thalia's things," Kris said quietly. "I'd hoped it wouldn't look this bad in the daylight."

Polly turned to face her. "What are you going to do?"

"I...don't know. I can't sell it as is. There'll be insurance money—the policy was paid ahead by the estate for a few more months, but I don't know if that will be enough to fully replace the cabin or not, much less the contents."

"Do you need a place to stay? I've got a spare bedroom."

"After all that's happened lately, I can't thank you enough for the offer. But I'd better stay close to the shelter. I'd be afraid to be too far away."

"You can't just pitch a tent out here."

"With the way things are going, a bear would probably carry it off—with me in it. Maybe I can set up a bed in the kennel office for a few nights, while I try to find a small travel trailer. Most of them have all the amenities, so I'd be set until I figured out what to do."

Polly tapped a finger at her lips. "I do have a friend who recently bought a bigger one. Maybe you could lease her old one for a while. It's a bit cozy, but it's clean and only a couple years old. Nice little kitchen, half bath—nice big awning."

"That new, it should be in good shape."

"She didn't use it that much, either." Polly glanced at her watch, then pulled a cell phone from her pocket and punched in a number. She walked around the remains of the cabin one more time as she talked, and when she came back she was smiling. "You're welcome to it for a month. After that, you two could negotiate for a sale, lease or just end the deal, no questions asked."

"Tell her it's a deal—sight unseen—and ask her when I can pick it up." Kris grinned. "I wasn't really looking forward to staying in the kennel—even for one night. The barking would drive me crazy."

"What about clothes? Food and so on?"

"One stop at the discount place on the edge of town will do it. A few jeans, sweatshirts and such, and I'll be set. In fact, I think I'll be heading into town to do just that—"

Polly looked over her shoulder. "Or maybe not. It looks like you have company from the Rocking R."

Sure enough, a familiar black pickup was rounding the last curve in the lane and heading straight for them. Carrie—no, it was Trace under the brim of that black hat.

From his height and the breadth of those shoulders, it couldn't be anyone else.

"I'd better be going, hon, so I can get cleaned up and get to the pet store. Do you need anything else? Will you be okay out here?"

"Fine. Absolutely fine. Thanks so much for your help, Polly."

"Don't you worry—things will work out. I just know they will." Polly gave her a quick hug, then got in her car and waved to Trace as she passed him.

Kris felt her mouth drop open when he pulled to a stop and slowly got out. First came a cane, then his left leg, which was fitted with some sort of complex, hinged metal brace.

"What happened?" she cried out, closing the gap between them.

He bent over to adjust something on the brace, and when he straightened, his faint, weary smile told her the answer without words.

"Oh, *no*. This is from that night when you helped me rescue Lucy, isn't it!" She reached him, wanting to give him a hug of thanks, hesitated, then she cast discretion to the winds and gave him a hug anyway. "I am so, so sorry."

He held back for a moment, then returned her embrace. "It wasn't just that night. Though," he added as he pulled away, "the midnight hike was probably the final straw. I've been in physical therapy three times a week. They said I'll be better than I was before, though—I've got a new therapist who says I should have been pushing the PT all this time."

"You should have told me. I could've helped drive you there, or something."

"It's okay. Carrie has been my chauffeur, for the most part."

She closed her eyes briefly as a wave of guilt rushed through her and landed like a heavy, wet blanket on her chest. It had been her fault, and then he had shut her out completely, even as a caring friend. "I never should've let you go with me that night."

"This is why I told Carrie not to say anything. And it *wasn't* your fault. It was my choice, and I did what I had to do. End of story. Now, I need to get to work."

"You're here to check out the fire?"

"To gather evidence, yes."

"I sure hope you find some answers. No one seemed to have any last night."

"We'll see."

"Well, I need to do all of my kennel chores, so I'll get out of your way. If you need anything, just yell."

"I will." He gave her a long, measuring look. "I most definitely will."

"Before I go—have you heard anything about Sam?"

"Nothing conclusive. He was in surgery last night, and was talking this morning. I understand he didn't see the face of the shooter."

She'd hoped Sam could do a positive ID on the guy. "I think that same man shot at me, too. And if he's the one who let the dogs free, we'd be that much closer to solving the whole situation."

She looked so hopeful, so eager to find the person behind her troubles…or was she?

Trace tried to shove his personal feelings aside as he slowly walked the perimeter of the cabin, then awkwardly hunkered down and began sifting through the remains. A total loss like this one usually made an investigation harder because there was so little to go on…no remaining walls to show char patterns, the collapsed walls were harder to discern.

But one thing he knew for sure—this fire had been so intense that it was definitely arson. The accelerant—probably kerosene—had been liberally doused throughout, and then the fire had been started in multiple locations around the house for an even, fast burn.

From what his pals on the volunteer fire department squad had said last night, this had been a fully involved fire long before they ever arrived. They'd only stayed to ensure containment, and nothing more.

So…if an accelerant had been used, where were the containers? Had the arsonist tidily cleaned up his mess? Or had it all been tossed out in the weeds?

Banking on the weeds, Trace started slowly hiking around the meadow, searching through the heavy underbrush, then moving farther into the timber to check out any suspicious objects.

He'd made it three-quarters of the way around when he spied a long, slender shape lying on the tall grass, perhaps twenty-five feet from Kris's SUV. Even from a distance, he knew exactly what it was.

According to the sheriff, Kris had been found on the ground next to the SUV. Trace lifted his gaze to the ruined cottage. To the point where Kris had supposedly seen someone. And then to where Sam had been found.

The most likely scenario was what the sheriff already suspected. Arson. And the attempted murder of a deputy, who'd just happened to come upon the scene, and instantly become a major liability for the triggerman…or woman.

The sheriff had already thought it suspicious that Kris's beloved dog was conspicuously absent from the cabin on the one night it caught fire.

But what would be her motive?

Financial troubles and the lure of a windfall insurance check? Or arson—to frame someone and get them out of the way?

But no matter what his personal feelings were, the evidence Trace had found would go to the sheriff, and it would be out of his hands. *Let justice be served.*

He looked down at the grass, pulled on a pair of vinyl gloves and picked up Thalia Porter's Winchester—the one with her initials carved in the stock.

And prayed that Kris was as innocent as she seemed.

SEVENTEEN

Trace carefully placed the rifle in the backseat of his truck, locked the door, then continued his painstaking search of the area.

The soft, dried, bowed grasses of last summer were exposed now, freed from their snowy mantle to bob and sway in the wind…and to effectively hide ammo casings, footprints or other small bits of evidence.

After all the trucks and cars here last night, it would be impossible to pick out any particular tire treads from a suspicious vehicle.

And barring the squirrels, moose and bears that might have happened by, there were no witnesses. Except for Kris, who had reported seeing a tall person clear across the meadow. Bathed in the pulsing firelight this person had appeared to "glow" which only made him seem to be more figment than fact.

If such a person had been here, there was no sign.

With a sigh, Trace went back to the cabin site and gathered some samples, then made a labeled sketch of the wreckage and took a few dozen digital photos from all angles.

Satisfied, he headed for his truck to drop it all off before going to the kennel to announce his departure.

Kris must've seen him through a window, because she met him outside with a tentative smile. "Successful?"

"I got what I needed…and what was available."

"That doesn't sound good." She bit her lower lip. "Last night I got the impression that the sheriff considered *me* a possible suspect. I suppose it would make sense if you look back…a troubled childhood, bad marriage to a guy who was *real* trouble, financial troubles. Why not arson and toss in attempted murder? It would certainly make everyone's life easier," she added with a faint note of bitterness. "An easy way out."

"I'm not a criminal investigator for the sheriff's department. I only collect information regarding fires, and I evaluate that data for the county, or for the insurance companies who request a report." He hesitated, then added, "I did find a rifle, though. I'll have to turn it over to the sheriff for ballistics testing."

"A rifle?"

"Thalia's old Winchester was out in the grass."

She stared across the meadow, her arms wrapped tightly around her midsection. "So this bad guy must have known about the rifle already. He probably went inside the house to look for it before setting the fire." She spoke softly, almost to herself, and he had to strain to hear her. "He was inside the house…with my things, foraging around. The rifle was well hidden for safety…so it would have taken him a lot of time. If it hadn't been for the pizza, I would have been home much earlier. I might have surprised him."

"And then you might've been dead."

She shivered. "Where did you find it?"

"The rifle? Not far from your truck."

She drew in a shaky breath. "He was across the field when I saw him take aim. So that means he came clear around the field to plant that gun close by." She raised her troubled gaze to meet Trace's. "You don't even need to run ballistics on the rifle and the round that hit Sam. They'll match. Otherwise, that guy wouldn't try to plant the rifle close to me in hopes there'd be a murder charge."

He looked at her, truly looked at her, and realized that it would be impossible to think she could be guilty.

Whatever the evidence might show, her words were filled with quiet honesty, but coupled with a sense of inevitability that things would be out of her hands.

"Shell casings," he said.

"What?"

"Show me exactly where you were standing when you saw that guy take aim."

She moved to her SUV. Studied the ground, then moved closer to the back wheels. "About here."

"Where was the guy with the rifle?"

She lifted a hand, pointed to the far edge of the meadow. "About there."

"Okay. I'm going to walk in a straight line until I get there. Yell out if I veer one way or the other." He looked over his shoulder at her, smiled and started walking. "If we can find any shell casings, we might come up with fingerprints on them—which could ID your man."

Her eyes opened wider with wonder, though he guessed it was as much at his show of faith in her as at his idea. "A little to the left—no, the right. Straight ahead."

He made it across the meadow and turned. "Here?"

"Farther."

He moved ahead another ten feet. "Here?"

"More—almost to those pines. *Stop.*"

"Okay, now the fun begins. Come on over and I'll give you a pair of gloves, too. This'll still be like finding a grain of sand on a beach."

She hurried over, tugged on the gloves and dropped to her hands and knees, carefully parting the weeds.

He rocked back on his heels. "Let's get a system going. Shoulders parallel and almost touching. We can traverse this little area and make sure we don't miss anything."

"Great idea. Thanks."

A half hour later his knee was screaming in agony and he had to stand up. "We've been through most of this. Are you *sure* he was right here?"

She nodded decisively as she moved, closer to the line of trees and brush rimming the meadow. "Hey— I think I found it!" She parted the soft grass and revealed a gleaming brass casing.

"I'll get it—the less we touch it, the better." He gingerly picked it up using a fold of the plastic bag and dropped it in a small plastic bag. "This is going to the sheriff with the rifle, and I'm leaving right now. Will you be okay? Do you want to come along?"

"I'll be fine. I need to take care of all the shelter animals and let Bailey out for a run."

Trace stood up, then helped her to her feet. Their eyes collided, their gazes held…and the sudden, unexpected urge to kiss her nearly took his breath away. "I believe in you," he whispered, pulling her close for an embrace. "This will be over soon."

Her hair smelled of lemons and sunshine and something that was uniquely her own, and he held on a moment longer, not wanting to let her go.

She must have felt the moment, too, because when they stepped away, her eyes were shimmering and her cheekbones were brushed with a delicate hint of pink.

"We're going to talk about this when I return," he said. "I promise."

"I'll hold you to that, too." She laughed and pointed a stern finger toward his truck. "Hurry, so you'll get back sooner."

He hesitated at the door of his truck as a sudden feeling of uncertainty washed through him. "Come along with me," he urged. "Please."

She rolled her eyes. "I'm a big girl. It's broad daylight. And believe me, there's nothing left to steal out here. I should be just fine."

Grinning, Kris watched Trace drive away. What *was*

that just a minute ago? A connection that was warm, and loving and filled with promise…and out of the blue.

She might've thought she'd imagined it, except she'd seen the stunned expression in Trace's eyes and knew his reaction had matched her own.

It was as if that contact had brought forth a rush of intensified emotions that had been lingering, just below the surface, for the right moment to catch fire—though maybe that was an unfortunate analogy right now.

She turned for the kennels, feeling as if she could do a few somersaults on the way there—

And found herself staring up at a tall, unkempt man with shaggy dark hair, a snarl and one very, very big gun. An odor of stale beer and sweat surrounded him like a dank cloud. He looked familiar, and yet…

"Who are you?"

"Ain't that sad. You go about destroying lives, and you don't even recognize the person you've cut down."

At his words she realized who he was—Harvey Bascomb. She'd seen him once when he was angry. She'd never seen him like this—enraged. Crazed. She took a small step back. Then another.

"You have *any* idea of what you did?" he roared, sending the dogs in the kennel into a furious round of barking. "Any idea at all?"

His white polo shirt was filthy, his baggy tan slacks were cinched tight at the waist. Light colors. Colors that might reflect that pulsing glow of a fire.

"W-were you here last night?"

He swore softly, the words oily and venomous, sliding over her flesh in a way that made her skin crawl. "Now, what do *you* think? There was a deputy here—and I'll bet he remembers me *real* good."

"That was Sam Martin. Didn't you look before pulling the trigger? He's a *relative* of yours."

The cold, dead glitter in the man's eyes didn't waver. "Then I guess he's just collateral damage."

If this man didn't care about his own flesh and blood, she had no illusions about her own future. She blinked and swallowed hard as she took another minute, sliding a step back, praying he wouldn't notice.

"Going somewhere? I don't *think* so." His hand snaked out and grabbed her wrist in a viselike grip that he twisted until she cried out and fell to her knees, breaking his hold.

She staggered to her feet, her attention riveted on the rhythmic flexing of his fists.

This morning she'd fed the dogs and opened up their outside runs. Now the agitated animals were nervously pacing their enclosures, whining, their tails tucked between their legs.

"Shut up," Bascomb shouted, gesturing angrily.

Some of the dogs cowered, but the rest started barking, the deafening chorus drowning out his next words.

Just another couple steps and she could reach the front latches of those pens. In the ensuing melee, could she run for safety?

"You fool." He spat the words, the veins in his neck distending. "Thanks to you, word will get out about the county taking my dogs. My reputation will be ruined. No one will bring their hunting dogs to me for training now…not anymore. A lifetime of honors—wasted. I was ready for a big comeback and you destroyed it all."

He reeled a bit on his feet, and at that moment she whirled around, ducked and slammed her hands upward against the dog-run latches, hitting two at a time as she ran down the line.

The dogs burst out of their pens, barking and snarling, clearly agitated by his belligerent behavior. One of them, a pit bull mix, went after Bascomb's ankle and he screamed.

She didn't look back. She ran into the kennel office. Slammed and locked the door. Then she spun toward the inner door leading to the dog pens.

A tall, vacant-eyed man stood in her way, big and solid as an oak, leering at her. "Now, we get to play."

His voice was high and thin, with an odd note of hysteria, and it could not have come from such a hulking frame.

But as he advanced slowly toward her, she knew this was no joke…and if she couldn't escape, this would be the day that she died. She could see it in his eyes.

EIGHTEEN

Uneasy, Trace stepped on the accelerator as he turned onto the highway leading to Battle Creek. The guy who'd shot Sam was probably behind the other troubles at Kris's place. If so, he was rapidly escalating.

Trace had gone back, trying to convince her to come with him rather than stay alone. *You'll be back in an hour*, she'd said. *It's broad daylight, and I've got Bailey here. I can't expect you to be my babysitter 24/7.* She'd been so adamant that he'd finally left to get the new evidence in the sheriff's hands.

Evidence Trace prayed would resolve this situation once and for all.

In a perfect world there'd be a match between the microscopic rifling marks inside the barrel of Thalia's rifle and the round that had been buried in Sam Martin's chest. And the shell casing in Trace's possession would yield clear fingerprints matching a set in AFIS, the national fingerprint registry.

But what if the casing had been left by someone

who'd simply happened to be in the area weeks earlier?

A false lead would delay identification of the real shooter. *And if he isn't caught, he'll go after her next. Please, Lord...help me here. Help us find this guy before it's too late.*

If only she'd come to town with him.

His nagging feeling of unease grew with each passing mile, but now he was practically to the outskirts of town and could see the one and only four-way stop sign on the main drag through town.

The sheriff's office was a quarter mile beyond that. It wouldn't take long....

But again, an inner voice urged him to go back.

He hesitated. Then pulled the truck off the highway onto the shoulder amid a boiling cloud of dust. When it cleared, he checked for traffic from both ways and floored the accelerator as that inner feeling became something close to panic.

She'd insisted on staying back there.

But how foolish was that? If someone wanted to get at her, this would be the perfect time—with no one to protect her. No witnesses.

He hit the steering wheel with the palm of his hand, then fished for his cell phone and dialed 911.

Kris stared at the hulking man in front of her and back up along the edge of the desk, blindly groping at her side for any possible weapon, her heart hammering against her ribs.

Behind her, the older Bascomb kicked open the locked door, shattering the doorframe and sending splinters flying. A miasma of sweat, tobacco, and stale alcohol filled the small room as he took a step inside.

Time—she needed time.

If she could only stall long enough, maybe the phone would ring and she could scream for help…or someone might think it odd if there was no answer at all.

Or a visitor might stop.

Or Trace might come back.

Please, God, send him back.

"At least tell me," she said, scrambling for a diversion. "W-why you let all of the dogs loose?"

"You stole ours, so we got our best ones back. Can't build a big reputation again without good stock."

"B-but what about all the records on the dogs? The county has copies. They'll figure it out. If…if you just leave now, nothing will happen. I won't say *anything.*"

Bascomb leered at her. "After I torch this building, no one will ever know which dogs died in the fire, so nothin' will point to me. There'll be no proof I was even here. And you won't be alive to tell anyone different."

"The sheriff will know. He'll find dogs at your place—"

"Save it. Me and the boy are leaving town anyway." He started toward her, the veins in his neck bulging, his face dark with hatred.

Already knowing the answer but praying for extra seconds, she took a steadying breath. "And y-you're the one who burned down Thalia's cabin?"

"Too bad Sam had to get in the way…and you, too." He leaned in close, his breath foul. "Retribution. Right, Leonard? Payback, fair 'n' square."

The younger man nodded.

"You got everything you wanted, then. Just let me go. Please."

Bascomb tossed back his head and laughed. "Right."

When he looked away for a moment, she rapidly scanned the room for anything—any possible weapon.

Her gaze fell on a shoebox of several bark collars donated to the shelter. Next to them, because the office was still in such disarray, was a pile of bandaging material and a torn box holding several slim, stainless-steel scalpels. She palmed one, careful of its incredibly sharp blade, and turned sideways to keep both men in view.

Leonard was taller, younger, with an eerie presence that suggested he might veer dangerously into the macabre if given a chance. The elder Bascomb's anger was palpable.

Please, God, give me a sign…tell me what to do.

The loose dogs outside had stayed close. Now, they started the agitated sort of barking that signaled a visitor. *Let that be someone coming. Please…let that be someone coming.* Someone big and burly and strong.

But what if it was a sweet young mother with children?

Or Trace was walking straight into a trap?

Bascomb's eyes narrowed as he listened to the dogs outside. "It's probably time for us to be on our way, so maybe we'd better make this short and quick. Leonard?"

Leonard started toward her. Bascomb moved closer, too, his hands clenched.

She spun around and slashed low, catching Leonard across the thighs.

He screamed in surprise and pain, his hands clutching his jeans. Bascomb lurched forward and grabbed her from behind, his breath hot and moist and fetid at her ear. She struggled, trying to kick and bite, but he clamped her to his chest with one arm, his other hand sliding up to tighten around her neck.

"I'm bleeding to death here!" Leonard screamed. "Kill her!"

She fought, then let herself turn to deadweight in his grip until he had to drop the hand at her neck to catch her. She clawed for anything within reach. *Anything.*

The small cardboard box tipped over, dumping the shock collars on the table. Blindly, she grabbed for one. Her fingers curled around each one of the thick, sturdy leather collars with long prongs and she fumbled at the tiny switch, praying she'd turned it on and that the batteries were good. *Please, God.*

She twisted in Bascomb's arms and rammed the

prongs against the bare flesh that held her. He yelped in pain and anger, releasing her just long enough for her to wrench herself from his grip and race for the open front door.

She met a solid wall of strong male. Muscled arms grabbed her, gently set her aside. "Go. Out to my truck. Call the cops and lock the doors. *Now.*"

For once in her life she didn't ask questions. She ran.

Kris shivered as Sheriff Carpenter and his deputies stuffed the two Bascombs into separate patrol cars. Trace hovered nearby, clearly ready and more than eager to help.

With talent reminiscent of his rodeo days, he'd had both of the Bascombs tied up in no time flat, then he'd guarded them intently until the patrol cars finally arrived.

It's over…it's over. Thank You, God…it's over.

The litany had been running through her head for the past forty-five minutes while she waited for help to arrive, gave her statement and watched the officers prepare to haul the two men off to jail.

When the patrol cars finally rolled away, her knees almost buckled with relief. Trace moved instantly to her side. "You should have stayed warm in my truck all this time. You must be freezing."

She shuddered, rubbing her upper arms against a deep chill that had nothing to do with weather. "I *had* to stay out here. I had to make sure that they were really taken away."

"You still could've watched from the truck," he teased. "You would've had a ringside view."

"Not enough. I still can't believe what they did. Even down to spreading all those rumors, wanting to drive me out of town."

"But it's the end of the road for them now." His warm, dark eyes filled with unspoken emotion as he looked down at her. "In a way, maybe they did me a favor."

"What?" She knew, but she asked anyway, just needing to hear the words.

"I've been so caught up in the past. Guilt. Regret. Anger at myself. Dwelling on how I should've been able to save my buddy's life. I failed him, and I guess I failed my fiancée somehow, too. After all that, the last thing I wanted was to risk finding myself close to anyone else."

"I know. It's easier that way."

"But then I met you, and I started to think." His mouth tipped into a rueful smile. "I guess God was sending me a wake-up call. I always knew that He'd forgiven me, but I still needed to hand all that baggage over to Him and forgive myself."

She laughed, a musical sweet sound that touched his heart. "I know exactly what you mean. There's no sense staying in the past when the present might be absolutely wonderful."

"Exactly. And seeing how close I came to losing you made me realize that without taking chances, I could lose a gift He has brought into my life. You." He hesitated, his eyes searching hers, then he kissed her, his firm mouth gentle and warm. Little ribbons of delight unfurled around her heart as the kiss went on and on, sending tingles of joy clear down to her toes.

"Mmm," she murmured, when that beautiful kiss ended. "I really think I'm going to enjoy Montana—even more than I ever expected."

EPILOGUE

"Well—what do you think now?" Carrie grinned at Trace and Kris, then turned back to study the framing of the new cabin. "Is it what you expected?"

"That and more," Kris breathed. She leaned against Trace's side, savoring the warm strength of his arm around her shoulders as she surveyed the grassy meadow.

Now strewn with early spring wildflowers, a riot of color waved in the gentle breeze—tiny yellow bells, snowy spring beauties veined in pink, delicate purple shooting stars.

"Even after all the fire debris was hauled away, the site looked like an open wound," Kris continued. "Now it feels like a wonderful new beginning."

New beginnings, in more ways than one.

"The sheriff says he's bringing Sam out this afternoon to see it, now that he's doing better," Trace said. "I hear he might even be able to go back to work in another month."

"I still feel badly, knowing he got shot while protecting my property." Kris shuddered. "Bascomb didn't even care that he'd shot his own blood relative."

"You won't have to worry about him any longer." Trace gave her an extra hug. "He'll be looking at a good twenty years just for arson, not to mention breaking and entering, theft and assault. Add that to shooting a police officer, and I don't think he'll ever see sunshine and freedom again. His son will be going away for a long time, as well."

The last few months had brought other changes, too.

Allan's buddies were back in jail after violating their parole, and Allan was back in Idaho, well aware of the repercussions should he ever violate a new Montana-based no-contact order.

And Trace and Kris had fallen deeply, irrevocably in love.

Carrie beamed. "I still can't believe that you're staying here after all."

"I don't need to change careers to find what I need. I found what makes me happiest—this beautiful place and a job I love. It's like God led me through a lot of dark times in my life, just so I could be right here, right now, and know enough to appreciate it." *Thank You, Lord.*

Trace laughed. "Okay…the mountains. Your job. Anything else?"

"Hmm. Let me think." She stepped into his open arms for a long kiss that sent shivers down her spine. "Nothing—unless it's the perfect cowboy."

He kissed her again. Longer this time, a kiss filled with all the promises of a life together. The chance to grow old with someone she loved with all her heart. A future she'd never believed possible such a short time ago. Blessings beyond measure.

And then, her joy and thankfulness overflowing, she kissed him back.

* * * * *

Dear Reader,

Welcome to the Montana Rockies! I hope you enjoyed your stay, through the pages of this book. If you'd like to visit again, the first book in this series was *Final Exposure*, which was out in September 2009. The next will be out in June 2010.

I also hope you enjoyed the story of Kris and Trace, two people who needed to overcome troubles from their past lives in order to finally be happy and capable of falling in love. Trace had been shouldering a burden of guilt over the death of his best friend. And healing emotionally from a childhood tragedy was Kris's key to being able to lead a full and abundant life—the life God wants for all of us.

One of my late father's favorite Bible verses was *Romans* 8:28: "All things work together for good for those who love God, who are called according to His purpose." It's one of my favorites, too, because it's such a wonderful reminder that with faith in God, life can unfold in mysterious and wonderful ways that we can't even fathom…even when there are hardships along the way. If you are still struggling with emotional trauma from tough times in your own life, it's my hope that perhaps this story has offered some encouragement. Turning to God in prayer can make all the difference!

Wishing you blessings and peace,

QUESTIONS FOR DISCUSSION

1. Kris no longer has family ties, and she longs for that sort of connection. Have lost or damaged family ties affected your own life? How? Is there any way these relationships could be recovered?

2. As a young girl, Kris was traumatized by the brutal murder of her friend, and it has continued to affect her into adulthood. Have you experienced traumatic incidents in your own life? What is the best way to help a child—or an adult—suffering in this way?

3. Kris's former husband still wants her to give him money, saying he desperately needs her help, and he isn't above threatening her in order to get what he wants. How should she deal with him?

4. Kris and Trace both pray for help during this story. How are their prayers answered? Have you prayed for help in your own life? How were your prayers answered?

5. Kris initially believes that since God didn't step in to save Laura, then surely He won't care about Kris's well-being, either. Why do terrible things sometimes happen to good people? What does the Bible say about this?

6. Kris is harmed by vicious rumors circulating about her past. Have you ever been the subject of rumors…or have you passed them along? Which of the Ten Commandments addresses this?

7. St. Francis of Assisi said, "If you have people who will exclude any of God's creatures from the shelter of compassion and kindness, you will have people who will deal likewise with their fellow human beings." Do you agree? Do you know of any pets that are being mistreated in your neighborhood? What should you do?

8. Trace feels responsible for the death of his best friend, and that guilt has proved to be a heavy burden. What would you say to him about guilt and forgiveness if you had a chance to help him?

9. Kris and Trace were believers before this story began, but events in the story brought them to a deeper level of faith. What events in your own life have affected your belief in God? What could you say to someone whose faith has been faltering?

10. Look up *Philippians* 4:6–7. How does this relate to the main characters at the end of the story? Could these verses apply to your own life?

Read on for a sneak preview of
KATIE'S REDEMPTION
by Patricia Davids,
the first book in the heartwarming new
BRIDES OF AMISH COUNTRY *series*
available in March 2010
from Steeple Hill Love Inspired®.

When a pregnant formerly Amish woman
returns to her brother's house, seeking forgiveness
and a place to give birth to her child,
what she finds there isn't what she expected.

*P*lease, God, don't let them send me away.

To give her child a home Katie Lantz would endure the angry tirade she expected from her brother. Through it all Malachi wouldn't be able to hide the gloating in his voice.

An unexpected tightening across her stomach made Katie suck in a quick breath. She'd been up since dawn, riding for hours on the jolting bus.

Her stomach tightened again. The pain deepened. Something wasn't right. This was more than fatigue. It was labor.

Breathing hard, she peered through the blowing snow. It wasn't much farther to her brother's farm. Closing her eyes, she gathered her strength.

One foot in front of the other. The only way to finish a journey is to start it.

She sagged with relief when her hand closed over the railing. She was home.

Home. The word echoed inside her mind, bringing with it unhappy memories that pushed aside her relief. Raising her fist, she knocked at the front door. Then she bowed her head and closed her eyes, grasping the collar of her coat to keep the chill at bay.

When the door finally opened, she looked up to meet her brother's gaze.

Katie sucked in a breath and then took a half step back. A tall, broad-shouldered Amish man stood in front of her with a kerosene lamp in his hand and a faintly puzzled expression on his handsome face.

It wasn't Malachi.

To read more of Katie's story,
pick up KATIE'S REDEMPTION
by Patricia Davids, available March 2010.

LARGER-PRINT BOOKS!

**GET 2 FREE
LARGER-PRINT NOVELS
PLUS 2 FREE
MYSTERY GIFTS**

Love Inspired®

SUSPENSE
RIVETING INSPIRATIONAL ROMANCE

Larger-print novels are now available...